ENVY

7 Deadly Sins Vol. 6

First published as a collection February 2019
Content copyright © Pure Slush Books and individual authors
Edited by Matt Potter

BP#00076

All rights reserved by the authors and publisher. Except for brief excerpts used for review or scholarly purposes, no part of this book may be reproduced in any manner whatsoever without express written consent of the publisher or the author/s.

Pure Slush Books
32 Meredith Street
Sefton Park SA 5083
Australia

Email: edpureslush@live.com.au
Website: https://pureslush.com/
Store: https://pureslush.com/store/

Original hand image copyright © Gerd Altmann
Cover design copyright © Matt Potter

ISBN: 978-1-925536-70-6

Also available as an eBook
ISBN: 978-1-925536-71-3

A note on differences in punctuation and spelling

Pure Slush Books proudly features writers from all over the English-speaking world. Some speak and write English as their first language, while for others, it's their second or third or even fourth language. Naturally, across all versions of English, there are differences in punctuation and spelling, and even in meaning. These differences are reflected in the work *Pure Slush Books* publishes, and they account for any differences in punctuation, spelling and meaning found within these pages.

Pure Slush Books is a member of the
Bequem Publishing collective
http://www.bequempublishing.com/

• Jason ARMENT • Melissa AUBURN • Gary BECK • Paul BECKMAN • Jim BELL • Mary BONE • Howard BROWN • Michael BROWNSTEIN • Elizabeth BUTTIMER • Patricia CARNEY • Steve CARR • Guilie CASTILLO ORIARD • Helen CHAMBERS • Carl CHAPMAN • Jan CHRONISTER • Darrell COGGINS • Sarah CONKLIN • Robert COOPERMAN • Carolyn CORDON • Linda M. CRATE • Tony DALY • John DAVIS • Sue DAWES • Holly DAY • Ruth Z. DEMING • Steve DEUTSCH • Bruce Louis DODSON • Damian DRESSICK • Judah ELI • Michael ESTABROOK • Tom FEGAN • Monica FERNANDEZ • Ann GABEL • Nod GHOSH • Alison Theresa GIBSON • Warren Paul GLOVER • Ken GOSSE • Claire HART • Jo HOCKING • Mark HUDSON • Susan HUEBNER • Pat HURLEY • Phillis IDEAL • Christine JOHNSON • Michaeleen KELLY • Jemshed KHAN • Eddy KNIGHT • John KUJAWSKI • Bruce LADER • Ron. LAVALETTE • Larry LEFKOWITZ • Mike LEWIS-BECK • Peter LINGARD • Alice LITTLE • JP LUNDSTROM • Reine MARAIS • Jackie Davis MARTIN • John MARTINO • Jan McCARTHY • Stephen MEAD • Todd MERCER • Karla Linn MERRIFIELD • Peter MICHAL • Miriam MITCHELL-BENNETT • Marsha MITTMAN • Ebony L. MORMAN • Michael Robinson MORRIS • Colleen MOYNE • Christie Munson MULLER • Piet NIEUWLAND • Pat O'CONNOR • Edward O'DWYER • Eileen M. O'REILLY • Pamela PAINTER • Carl 'Papa' PALMER • M PAUSEMAN • Melisa QUIGLEY • Stephen V. RAMEY • Stephanie REENTS • Aaron RETZ • Ruth Sabath ROSENTHAL • Michele SAINT-YVES • Gerard SARNAT • Dorin SCHUMACHER • Robert SCOTELLARO • Stephen SEABRIDGE • R Scott SEXTON • Mir-Yashar SEYEDBAGHERI • Beate SIGRIDDAUGHTER • Lloyd SIMON • Dan SPENCER • Lisa STICE • E. M. STORMO • Margaret SWART • Judith TAYLOR • Tim THOMPSON • Chloe TIMMS • Lucy TYRRELL • Kim WATSON • Michael WEBB • Jeffrey WEISMAN • Nan WIGINGTON • Allan J. WILLS •

Contents

1   Poetry

85   Prose | Fiction

231   Prose | Non-Fiction

Poetry

5	Changing Places	*Judith Taylor*
6	Home Sweet Home	*Gerard Sarnat*
8	He Da Man	*Ron. Lavalette*
9	The Chasm	*Elizabeth Buttimer*
10	Décor	*Todd Mercer*
11	Celebrity Celibacy	*Carl 'Papa' Palmer*
12	Ambush	*Michael Estabrook*
14	Eight-Layer Chocolate Cake	*John Davis*
15	Back to Earth	*Karla Linn Merrifield*
16	On the Platform	*Tony Daly*
18	It was envy back then	*Susan Huebner*
20	Winter Sports for Girls	*Lisa Stice*
21	fathers & daughters	*Linda M. Crate*
22	The Grapes of Envy	*Ken Gosse*
24	The Joneses	*Colleen Moyne*
26	Other Versions	*Stephen Mead*
28	Losing My Wits in Envy's Black Hole *Ruth Sabath Rosenthal*	
30	The Older Sister	*Robert Cooperman*
32	If at first you don't succeed, try, try again	*Mark Hudson*
36	A Parade on Oriental	*Piet Nieuwland*
38	as deep cold settles in	*Lucy Tyrrell*
40	Oblivia's Dilemma	*Michaeleen Kelly*
42	To the Woman Who Got Published Instead of Me *Jan Chronister*	

43	Evil Eye	*Patricia Carney*
44	The Lyricist	*Michele Saint-Yves*
46	A Vast Envy	*Darrell Coggins*
48	Claim It	*Margaret Swart*
49	Whisper to a Mason Jar	*Holly Day*
50	Envy Tableau	*Kim Watson*
52	Astride a Fiery Demon	*Howard Brown*
53	This is Why We Cannot Create Community	*Michael Brownstein*
54	Green, Green, Green	*Marsha Mittman*
56	Envy Is the Death of My Enemy Heart	*John Martino*
58	Envy	*Jemshed Khan*
60	Egocentric	*Bruce Louis Dodson*
61	Time to get sober	*Sarah Conklin*
62	Thou Shalt Not	*Ann Gabel*
63	Wolf-Pack	*Mary Bone*
64	Piano Envy	*Pat Hurley*
66	Hi-Fiction	*Judah Eli*
70	Masquerade	*Eileen M. O'Reilly*
72	Envy, It's Not	*R Scott Sexton*
74	Who Envies Who?	*Carolyn Cordon*
76	Child of Comparison	*Stephen Seabridge*
78	A.I. VI	*Gary Beck*
80	Sex Appeal	*Steven Deutsch*
82	Success Story	*Edward O'Dwyer*

Changing Places

Judith Taylor

It can happen

The girl who made fun
of the clothes you wore, passed down
from one sister and the next

threw her crusts at you
every lunch period

spat on your family's
Pontiac Grand Le Mans station wagon

Is now getting jeans for you
in The Gap ™

Change room.

Home Sweet Home

Gerard Sarnat

Not to make a big deal of it (and pleeease
do not let on to anyone else who might be
a bit jealous,

    or more likely think we're morons);
but my wife and I are just nomads
living in three homes, each successively littler,

that follow the migrations of our kids and theirs.
The first is the family plot in the forest: Albeit
not very large by Silicon Valley standards,

    still it's a light comfy country house
which has one of those gravel circular driveways
where Citroens parked, like in Truffaut New Wave

    flicks when I was a teen sophisticate.
I won't be writing any more about that one but
will about the others – plus photos. The second's

a small white beachcomber condo with everything
subservient to oceanfront views and writing. Lastly's
the studio apartment above a daughter's family garage.

    It's unclear now rounding the bend toward 70,
how our golden years'll play out though I'm sure
my final resting place will be reeeally tiny, dark.

He Da Man

Ron. Lavalette

I see all the women who follow him around;
follow him into restaurants and bars;
the ones who never leave before closing time;
the ones he gets to choose from; the one
he chooses: a different one every night.

I've seen the tips he leaves the barmaid;
watched him sign the tab, watched him
peel off half a dozen nice crisp twenties
just for good measure; watched the barmaid,
beaming, wishing she were off the clock.

I see him, always chauffeured everywhere,
climbing in and out of his spotless limo,
never having to worry about a schedule;
never opening a door for himself anywhere;
never the tiniest smudge on his tailored suit.

I could go for some of that; I could be
the king of the world on only the tiniest bit.
I could be in heaven if I could only have
the merest fraction of what he's got;
one day like his day, once or twice a year.

If only, if only, if only.

The Chasm

Elizabeth Buttimer

She nurses her envy like some people
feed a newborn by their breast
whose suckling takes nourishment
from their bones and body.
She believes in keeping that emotion
close to her vest, and harbors
a protective zeal for letting envy
propagate in darkness as she mulls
over and over the disparity
between them. The oceans of money,
comfort and status that lie like the crossing
of the Atlantic as a chasm.
They began at the same post but the race
took different turns and tumbles
which led to victory or defeat.
Now, all that is left is the rift,
the gulch that amasses before them
and ever-growing, ever-plumping
resentment that latches on and seeps all
her milk of human kindness.

Décor

Todd Mercer

We're a step slow and one shade toward lackluster
since the Joneses moved in on the green side of the fence,
next door. They have exquisite taste and cash to burn,
thus their borderline addiction to home improvement.
At this moment for example, Dick's adding fake shutters
outside their windows. Shutters that won't move.
Décor. It makes me sick but this enthralls my Jane.
She asks me (rhetorically): *Where is our loggia?*
Why no hanging garden of orchids and hibiscuses
and carnivorous plants? Jane is not a fan of second place,
or warming arthritic hands in the glow of neighboring fires.
When will we have a barbecue pit? How long must we suffer
without a kidney-shaped pool? Why the lack
of outdoor warming towers? There's no end to want.
Been forced into DIY projects every free moment.
Working on our house, I eye the Jones' Lamborghini,
parked on their freshly-resurfaced semicircular driveway.
One car from a fleet that Dick rarely uses, leaves sitting,
the model that I've wanted my whole adult life.
Jane and I play constant catch-up. We wake then work
on aspirations, on consumer goods collections
soon as we are dressed. The day's a-wasting, I say.
Otherwise we'll never match these maddeningly perfect people
who lack problems, as far as we can see from over here.

Celebrity Celibacy

Carl 'Papa' Palmer

Her laptop sits upon my pillow,
poems covering my side of our bed.

Jazz escapes her earphones as I lean
in for a quick peck on my cheek.

Her eyes return to her writings
as I exit unmissed to the den.

This same scene, nine months of
nights, sleeping on the couch.

I hold myself to blame, begged
her to come, read for open mike

and she loved it. Her first reading
wowed the audience, read again,

became a regular, joined poetry
groups, found her voice,

was asked to be the featured reader,
wrote more, read more, published,

working on her second collection,
poems covering my side of our bed.

Ambush

Michael Estabrook

"You flow like a river,"
exclaims my rival in ballroom dancing class,
turning my wife gently, yet surely,
beneath his long arm. She smiles
her pretty little-girl smile, obviously pleased
with her dancing, with herself
picking up this new move,
the rumba extended box step,
as easy as 1 – 2 – 3.

Her tall, handsome, debonair partner
frequently gazes past his bony, lanky,
gray-haired albatross of a wife
to watch my perfectly gliding dove,
confident and composed, swinging
and swaying as she cha-cha-chas with me.

But as much as he'd like to,
he can't have her,
he cannot have my beautiful wife.
I don't even want him looking at her
let alone dancing with her
not even for one minute.

But I must admit (it's me
being neurotic I'm sure) just for
a fleeting moment she seemed to flush
warm and pink and sweet as she turned
beneath his long arm,
as my senses stiffened
and my poor heart cringed beneath
the sudden cold sweat of potential ambush.

Eight-Layer Chocolate Cake

John Davis

Envy begins in a chocolate cake. Whether or not
we are allergic to chocolate or have an aversion

to chocolate, we have consumed chocolate
for birthdays or celebrations of freshened wishes.

Who hasn't bathed his or her body in chocolate lust?
Who hasn't faded into chocolate on a high mountain hike?

Mothers have made love after eating chocolate
and their chocoholic children whose lives

have succeeded, have swallowed chocolate
and supplied chocolate to welders of blunt and sharp swords.

In chocolate microscopes we see the moon is the heart and not
the home under our ribs. In chocolate dances we swing

the one that makes us moon crazy. The chocolate princess
or prince, kisses a chocolate lie along our scalps

and the world and the chocolate underworld collide in love
and we write chocolate verse so we can move our clocks ahead.

Back to Earth

Karla Linn Merrifield

Here, at Mound 33, lies an old woman,
arms folded with a bundle of bird-
bone needles tucked under her right
arm & wide river white clam shells
blanketing her last remains untouched
until the year I was born. Meeting
her here today as unsettled as she
again was resettled, as deeply buried
in myself as she was once excavated
to see light of day 1,500 years later,
I envy her repose after startling surprise,
her silence after such rude discovery.

On the Platform

Tony Daly

At the frost covered train station
she stood, watching her breath crystallize,
feeling the frigid brilliance on her lips,
inhaling the beauty engulfing her.

Then another came
with a coat of spun wool buttoned high,
providing protection against the bitter chill.
Shivering, as the cold began creeping in,
she dreamed of a coat to warm her.

Then another came
wearing a pink-knit hat, sparkling
with highlights of fallen snowflakes,
shining angelically in the morning radiance.
She dreamed of shining half so bright.

Then another came
with leather boots laced to knees,
sheltering feet from environmental harm.
She dug her toes into the crusted snow,
dreaming of fur-lined boots of her own.

Then the train came.
Slowly, one by one, the others boarded.
The boots, the hat, the coat were all
loosened or discarded behind frosted glass.
She dreamed of a place isolated and warm.

Then the train left,
taking with it all her dreams and wishes.
She stood, again, alone on the platform,
watching her breath escape and crystallize,
smiling with the frigid brilliance engulfing her.

It was envy back then

Susan Huebner

of her long blond hair
Barbie Doll figure
The sheer blinding brightness of her
head thrown back laughter
fuchsia-painted toenails
designer purses and jeans
she couldn't afford
In her hands a wooden spoon
became a magic wand
She found joy in her cooking
and served always with flair
I still remember that Easter dinner
succulent lamb roast
with crisped-perfect skin

Shiny men were drawn to her glow
men with sports cars and beach property
men who wore gold chains
and chomped on thick moist cigars
bought her fur coats and paid for
her downtown apartment

She was beautiful back then
A woman like so many others
who couldn't see beyond her mirror
beyond those who wanted her surfaces
while she searched for her soul
in reflections of vodka

while I didn't know better
than to wish I glowed like her

Winter Sports for Girls

Lisa Stice

When I was a kid, I wanted to ice skate
and I did. It became my obsession for a while.
When I readied myself for a single Salchow,
I imagined I looked just like Dorothy Hamill
because I really couldn't imagine any further.

But my daughter yawned through the 2018
figure skaters, made me switch the channel
when she claimed ice dancing burned her eyes.
She imagines herself flying feet-first down a luge,
taking curves at 87 miles per hour, then
the even more exciting head-first version
of the same. She imagines her head bobbing
in a bobsled, her snowboard flipping and spinning
18 feet above the half-pipe, landing, removing her helmet,
catching her breath, and wanting to do it all again.

fathers & daughters

Linda M. Crate

i am envious
of daughters
who have fathers
those who have never known
aching loneliness
which comes from never knowing
their true name,
and i envy
those deep strands and deep ties
i will never experience or know;
my father rejected me and my adoptive father
left me feeling lonely in a crowded room
even surrounded by people who
i love
more often than not i feel the absence
that comes from never knowing
a deep and natural love
every child should get the chance to embrace
in their youth.

The Grapes of Envy

Ken Gosse

Sour grapes, an ancient story,
covers every category.
Seven seas of allegory—
rivered roads of life's empory
leading down to Hell.

Resentment shows its many faces,
envy for the noble graces
others show in daily paces.
Your life shows its many traces
where from grace you fell.

Lust for sex and its advances
when you notice someone dances
outside of your own romances.
Envy dictates this enhances
stories that you'll tell.

Gluttonous, in famished mood
you yearn for more than your own food.
What others by hard work accrued,
in envy, you feel you're imbued
to steal what they sell.

Greed calls, "Gather all the gold!"
though it's not yours to have and hold,
to store for life until you're old—
but envy lasts till you're too cold
to drink it from your well.

Slothful, you want naught but rest
when work would put you to the test.
Though others, feathering their nest
to make their life and home the best,
in envy, you excel.

Wrath confirms that you are owed
the fruits which many others sowed
while travelling their hard-paved road.
But envy is both potent goad
and landlord where you dwell.

In pride, you claim you're great and tough,
with fortune, fame, and needful stuff.
No matter how you huff and puff
you don't hear praise—you hear rebuff.
The meek you would expel.

It's not a leisure, this desire,
but seizure of an inner fire.
Hell's furnace burns but can't inspire,
for envy cultivates your ire
until your final knell.

The Joneses

Colleen Moyne

Haute couture
carefully packed
into designer luggage,
they headed off to Mozambique
to bask in the rewards
of working fifty hours a week

Booked into a five-star resort,
the most expensive suite
but never quite good enough;
never able to meet
the expectations
of these self-labelled elite.

They grumbled to the concierge,
complained about the food
and nothing he tried
could appease them
or elevate their mood

and yet,
back at home,
they boasted to their friends
about the trip
and how much
it all cost them –
including every tip

and they settled back into routine
of their fifty-hour week
so they could go again next year
to somewhere
even more exotic
and unique.

Other Versions

Stephen Mead

Of me parade in my fears
of what you might dream.
I have seen their photos & the magnified
negatives. I have read their mash notes &
only in print (illiterate, tedious), does
the resemblance disappear.

Baby, am I too the carbon copy of some
long ago ghost's ache?
If so, bless the aggression of my jealous envy
working your clay flesh.

If only the soul were so malleable,
the mind, the heart.
All of mine is the Karma Sutra melting
in abandon beyond technique
in the creed of ironing your surgical scrubs:
open aortas full in our look.

Are your other loves as aware of such need
in our time, the passing headlines death
spectres of ink?

I put blindfolds on statues, red ribbons
on chests, black arm bands as custom
for the unseen purple-hearted legions of regimes.
I take your seed & wonder if it is spit mixed
with the liquor of another.

I iron, darling, I iron our scrubs
before we pass, doing duty, in the stalwart
wards of so many who are us:

wheeled pietas
pealing.

Losing My Wits in Envy's Black Hole

Ruth Sabath Rosenthal

> "...I'll find your wits again.
> Come, for I saw them roll
> To where old badger mumbles
> In the black hole."
>
> W. B. Yeats, *Who Stole Your Wits Away*

I ask you, where is my body of wit
That I, a writer of doggerel, so wish

To gain from feasting on Yeats'
Poetic feats?

Though devouring each and every line
Of his genius I seem to be growing, line

By waste-line, stanza by stanza, less and less
In status, in the process. Where is the genius

In that? The accolades and awards. Medals?
I would never so much as bold a wish for gold,

Silver, sterling enough for me; but if bestowed
Bronze, I would surely find it every bit as swell.

The word choices I crank out of my lexical well
Lauded far and wide would show that, beyond a shadow

Of doubt, I pen poems right on par with those
Of poets who have literally grown phat

On W. B.'s great wit.

The Older Sister

Robert Cooperman

I push Bonnie's wheelchair
through the local Safeway, alert
for anyone who might bump into us,
Mother's orders: "Protect your little sister."

though maybe you think my concentrated
frown, my hovering care should belong
to someone older, stronger than me:
a stick-thin girl, when other girls
already have curves and wear bras,
while I navigate my precious cargo.

Mother's drilled this duty into my head,
that, "We all have to sacrifice,
for Bonnie's sake."

And I don't mind, really I don't,
knowing I'm doing good
and that Bonnie will love me
as much as she can, forever;
but even I can tell something's missing
from my life that other girls
accept as if their gift from the world.

When the time comes, I'll leave
for college, and no one can stop me.
I won't ever come back, and I'll call
less and less often; then not at all.

Or, like a careless lab experiment,
I'll finally explode with: "Yes,
I know Bonnie's fragile as china;
but I'm your daughter too,
not a nursemaid whose name
you can't be bothered to get right!"

If at first you don't succeed, try, try again

Mark Hudson

When I heard the topic of Envy pop up, the first thing that popped in my mind was writing about envying the dudes who lost their virginity before me. It would've been funny, but it would've worked better with "lust."

But then my mind went way back to my adolescent years.

Everybody gave me crap in Jr. High, as they always do. I envisioned becoming the next Steven Spielberg, making world-famous movies, and they'd say, "Remember that clown Hudson from jr. high? Well, now he's a major film producer!"

Well, my plans didn't work out that way.

When I grew up there were two brothers named Belic, and the younger brother was named Roko. They were always popular, and I wasn't.

I remember I had some art contest I had to work on after school, and Roko was there working on it with me. That is how I got to know him. He was a talented artist, and so was I. I think I came in the art contest third place.

Years later, after dropping out of college, or perhaps failing miserably, I had to work at a miserable movie theatre minimum wage job. Everybody I ever went to school with saw me there, and said, "I'm going to school to be a dentist. I'm going to school to be a lawyer."

And then they would laugh at me.

The final blow was when someone came to the box office where I was working and said, "Did you hear about the Belic brothers? They're out in the Los Angeles area making movies. They're winning awards."

That was the final blow. I was ruined!

I lost my job at the movie theatre after ten years of service. I was able to get an apartment through disability, and so I was done with working. I earned a degree in creative writing from Columbia, and began to take art classes, which I've done ever since.

One Christmas break from art school, a
lady said, "You should rent this DVD, 'Happy'.
It's a movie I think you'd like.

I rented it that lonely, month-long break
from Christmas, and watched it. It was a
documentary on happiness, what makes people
happy, the countries where people are the
most happy.

As I watched it, and saw these people,
whole countries of happy people, I cried I
was so envious. This area has so many terrible
memories for me, and I always wanted to leave.

Then they showed a Jr. High boy, who
said, "I am the shortest boy in my class, and
my peers used to make fun of me because
I was the shortest kid in my class! Then
I won the limbo contest, and I was the hero!"

And in the next scene, the kids are
carrying him above their head, like a hero!

I wept, because I have a nephew who
is short, and I hoped he would never be
made fun of the way I was as a kid.

And in grade school, in real life,
my nephew entered a limbo contest, and won!

The movie was amazing. It was beautiful. Then I looked at the credits.

Guess who did it?

The Belic brothers!

When I went to Columbia College, I wanted to study film animation. But it didn't work out. So I switched my major to creative writing.

The rest is history.

I don't want to envy anybody, and I envy nobody. We are all so painfully human, and we all have a story worth telling.

And as I approach another long lonely Christmas break from art school, I have plenty of writing projects to work on. This may be the best Christmas of all!

A Parade on Oriental

Piet Nieuwland

As the Inter-islander makes its way in, the world moves past me and a ferry crosses to Eastbourne

In the oceanic amniotic fluid the biting fish are tiny as One News interviews on the state of the state of the calm beneath which intercontinental tension builds

A child in stroller takes his grandfather for a walk as a sweating grimacing grin of runners pad past, a tattoo of pastel t-shirts and lycra shorts

With pink legs an orange-billed oystercatcher fossicks the foreshore amongst kelp and shells and piles of human waste that whales mistake for squid

A pair of purple jandals enviously awaits the return of their bare feet who have wandered off to a Glamaphones concert

I walk the blue arrowed path of an interactive marathon sponsored by Powerade where runners wear earphones and Fitbit devices so personal biodata can be monitored and broadcast to a global audience on Netflix

A red-hatted kayaker escorts a yellow buoy towed by a violet-capped swimmer and this all becomes a variety of mobile rainbow without the usual arc

Ministry of Funny Runs staff, at pace, breathing hard, snake along the path in their unique individual styles, as does a Chinese conversation with a Duolingo accent

E-bikers pass with broad it's so easy smiles and a squeeze of lime-scooters slip on by

A derailleur of cyclists zip in a fluoroblour as harakeke pods throb

At the yacht club under looming cumulonimbus anvils, race information has not yet been logged in the start box

Office crystals shimmer in tetragonal masses beneath a raggedly torn skyline

The harbor eyes a frontal molasses of cold air and downpours with hail now

There are still no fish on the way back to the bus stop, just the wet hiss and splash of cars

And the sea still only sees with mirrors

as deep cold settles in

Lucy Tyrrell

for days, mercury shrinks
near minus thirty-something.
Nostrils twinge and prickle,
and rosy cheeks and fingers burn.
Breaths of curled huskies
frost-freeze on fur and straw.
Stove gobbles bags of pellets.
Truck turns over with reluctance—
metal-on-metal scraping,
power steering fluid red on snow.

Aurora banners float in ribbons
packaging dusk-dim sky.
Moose lumber about with thick
hides of bristly hair—leaving track-paths
from their willow rambles.
Great gray owl skims the spruce,
lifting its bulk noiselessly with ragged-tipped
feathers—dark solemn parka.
Gray jays glide-fly to places they remember—
survival cached in crevices.

Tiny chickadees, barely a whisper
of weight, must eat, ravenous
against the cold night.
I don't envy such desperate appetites—
living seed to seed, larva to larva,
but maybe they know nothing
of risk and consequences—they call,
whistle cheerfully, winging
among birches bent with snow—
as deep cold settles in.

Oblivia's Dilemma

Michaeleen Kelly

Oblivia began her unique version of compare and contrast,
walking silently in single file
with other more confident kindergarteners,
her normal condition of fantasizing
jarred by her noticing of the other class' toy emporium.

Shiny firetrucks that could seemingly put out
the naughty boys' pyrotechnic antics.
Her own class' uninspiring firetrucks
whistles and bells free
And she was almost ready to give up on play entirely
when she sensed that the exhausted dolls in her room
couldn't even inspire maternal feelings in new mothers.

Later the paranoid silence of her sixth grade classroom
produced by Sister Bonafiglia's stick-wielding dramas
gave her the chance to imagine
the delights of students next door,
in their experiencing tantalizing learning adventures,
while she toiled away at dreary, redundant ditto sheets,
and reviewed times tables already second nature
and easy new spelling words.

Eighth grade found her ready to make a Faustian deal
to win back the focus of Matthew Tomaszewski,
no longer impressed with her spelling bee wins,
his eyes now glued to the squiggling body
of curvaceous Marilyn Mazurek,
squirming at the intolerable oak and metal desks,
hearing nothing about the correct answers
to diagramming sentences.

Needing to believe that perfection had to exist somewhere,
but realizing that existing in reality required critical vigilance
over one's self and its meager efforts and accomplishments,
only a staggering epiphany,
say, an invitation to joy,
could get Oblivia to cross over
to the side of the green grass growers
and begin to fertilize her own outpourings.

To the Woman Who Got Published Instead of Me

Jan Chronister

I have a hard time picturing you down on your knees
wiping away pee stains like I'm doing right now.

I scrub hard enough
to spill the dish of rice
my feng shui friend told me
to put on the tank lid.
It will bring good luck she said
keep positive energy
from flushing down the toilet.
I'm not sure this works
when almost all the rice has been
transported away by mice
but she tells me it's the intention that counts
the deliberate placement of
recommended artifacts.

When I'm done sweeping up rice
I flush, forget my rag
is in the bowl. Hopefully
it won't plug up the drain.
I've had enough good luck for one day.

Evil Eye

Patricia Carney

Disarming the Beauty of her sapphire sphere,
unblinking and dried-out like a peeled grape,
the evil eye envied such pretentious riches,

mentally robbing the orb for her own bauble.
Still, the Beauty held her equine neck erect
more beautiful for the imaginary disrobing

refusing to relinquish any grace to old roaming
eye of her beholder or bow to the envy.
Stepping on, the leg emerged from skirt slit,

cut from thigh to the ankle, a tall stiletto, sling-
back straps, emerged; she walked on, nose tilt
up as evil eye imaginatively dis-footed her stilettoes.

As if now barefoot, her striding long, she embraces
even more elegantly than when shod her arching
foot, curling as on fine white sand of shallow shore,

reclaiming the curve of her rounded buttocks–
backside offered to possessor of old evil eye.

The Lyricist

Michele Saint-Yves

Who does not want to be the one amongst all
who writes   that strand of a song
that lyric that everyone recalls?
The
'blackbird singing in the dead of night'
'there's a lady who's sure that all that glitters is gold'

Is it not our birthing duty
to honour the ancestral umbilical memory
by being better on this Earth?
As   longest life ever for learning
                    information never more
The
social systems they conceived still in place
technology dreamt of in their story.

All of this, just.

Is not the ghostly full moon true north
above the   true west ducking of the last of the sun
below the   sea stretched horizon
a talisman?   Janus's shadow:
The
indigo-peach lining of the east
grey-blue clouding of the south
inbetween-ing of birds returning to settle:

Asking us, why.

Why aren't we envious of the confidence of birds?
The
white streamers of cockatoos
tandem-parachuting of rainbow lorikeets
trapeze antics of piping shrikes
tile-snuggling of doves.

For in their cooing, screeching, trilling and *cackawwwahh*
do they not emit a warning to loss of our song?
Our collective amnesia of the lyrics to our communal anthem?
The
'should auld acquaintance be forgot and never brought to mind'
'and from your lip she drew a Hallelujah.'

A Vast Envy

Darrell Coggins

Your barbed clasp ferments

guarded with doubt
slipshod against my skin
you enclose my thoughts

At first simmering

acidic with craving
coursing through my veins
boiling over –

turning and returning
you blindfold revenge

Convoluted between
emptiness and fullness

I shield a version of myself

Squeezed in as you move
closer –

undressed up
sometimes vulnerable
at moments strong

your ulcerous clasp
hungers for more

Ineradicable –
tentatively scraped across

the intensity of what
you solicit and plunder
at first an itch –

soon becomes a burn

Claim It

Margaret Swart

Travelers beget luggage,
generations of generic
dark swirling hunks,
throbbing around
a clattering carousel.

Arriving at destination,
I applaud owners of Disney Princess
& Star Wars bags, easy to pluck
from that homogenous ocean
of black bergs.

Before my next journey
I'm getting something chartreuse,
buoy orange or pulsating purple.
Let the conventional be envious
of my garish display—

as me and my bag
roll spritely away.

Whisper to a Mason Jar

Holly Day

I'm in love with the little midges
that dance in the sunlight, their green wings
fluttering so quickly that they seem suspended in mid-air.
When I die, I want to become a creature like that
cavorting in sunbeams and buffeted by the wind.

I love the little spiders, too, tiny, bright
transparent and gelatinous but full of so much potential.
Just to know that I could grow from a pinprick
a spot on a piece of paper
into a hairy brute that sends housewives screaming
to the top of chairs, a bird-killer,
something with venom powerful enough
to stop a man's heart
I could wind my dreams about that.

I love the fireflies the best, though
blinking serenades across the water
disguising themselves as perfectly ordinary brown beetles
only unfurling their secret starlight at night.
I am also a firefly. I know
there is potential for sunshine inside me as well,
there is an unexpected brilliance
just waiting to explode.

Envy Tableau

Kim Watson

Once upon a time
when placed upon a
gilded pedestal –
the King of his world –
self-proclaimed and famed
for knowing it all –

fell from grace – replaced
his independence
with doctor visits –
surgeries – back, knees –
disabilities
erode stature – dimmed

apocalyptic
views – obsessed with news
of dissention – not
to mention jaded –
friends slowly faded
into their own lives.

He no longer thrives
on calls for advice –
trapped by the four walls
of fractured choices –
clinging to freedom
and envied by none.

Astride a Fiery Demon

Howard Brown

Astride a fiery demon, those smitten with
envy cruise through the world longing for
things that, by right, are not their own.

Their polarity of vision a true enigma, as they
clamor after the possessions of others, yet are
seemingly blind as to what they already have.

But, inevitably, the great Leviathan proves to
be a fickle mount and, with a simple twist of
its tail, eventually casts them each aside.

And rumor has it that somewhere in the nether
regions a special hell lies waiting for the
covetous: one of ice and water, rather than fire!

This is Why We Cannot Create Community

Michael Brownstein

– Because USA President Donald Trump said:
My followers are very passionate.

There is no passion in being a racist,
only the slick needle of anger from envy.
Notice I didn't say sick needle. I didn't say
necessary needle as in tetanus shot. I didn't
say inoculation or protection from.
Nor did I say a preventive measure
or a remedy for what is happening right now.
No, I used the words "slick needle" as in
blisters from stress or inability to thrive
even as you thrive and walk and talk,
but don't talk, don't think beyond the porch,
only know the sick needle of anger from an envy
you cannot put in words because envy
comes from a place you want to be
if only you could find your way away from it.

Green, Green, Green

Marsha Mittman

I envy
    My best friend so –
    Her beauty, perfect body
    And complete elegance.
    How she enters a room
    And everyone instantly
    Falls in love with her

I envy
    Her strong independence
    And ability to set limits –
    She decides with whom
    She wishes to associate
    And *she* draws the lines
    That cannot be crossed

I envy
    The lifestyle she's crafted
    Having every need met
    Every whim fulfilled
    With never a care

I envy
    The sound of her voice
    And communication skills.
    But most of all I envy
    Her ability to listen and love

I envy
    The one and only
    The absolutely fabulous
    Please may I be reincarnated as
    My cat, Princess

Envy Is the Death of My Enemy Heart

John Martino

I came to you in a blur
of fanatic adoration,
Double Fantasy under
my wing, silver marker

for the name's fixation.
One fast and final scrawl.
The walrus was never Paul.
Across the universe, all

the stars align in a constellation
of two. I was no one you knew,
no one you saw, merely a sudden
"Pleased to meet you. . ."

Self blown loose from a revolving cloud.
Eight days a week I plowed
the part, brokered by a lonely heart.
Just another face in the crowd

on the LP's cover art. Now,
I am thee as you are me and we
are the fascination of the masses,
twin halos glinting off

a pair of round-rimmed glasses.
Imagine all the people
thinking you/seeing me.
Sky of blue and sea of green.

Envy

Jemshed Khan

Midafternoon, Mr. Henderson lets us
romp through the playground.

We race through drizzle to the schoolyard toilets,
elbow and jostle ourselves inside

to unzip before the common stall.
Ian pisses the brick wall first,

higher than his head. Suddenly it's all contest
to top the urinal,

until Henderson barges in to jetting rivulets, dribbling walls,
crossed swords.

He's a wicked Christian when punishing sin.
We zip up fast. He scowls,

looking for an ear to grab, a boy to march
to the headmaster's paddle

as if Queen and Country depend upon civil aim
and porcelain.

Then he pauses. We stop and stare. Lads, lads.
He shakes his head, grins

as if remembering.

Egocentric

Bruce Louis Dodson

Joy of feeling better than the rest
and fear of being like them
yin yang trap of love and hate
both war and peace
the dance of opposites.
Where there is light
there must be dark to see
illusions.

As real as it can be.

Time to get sober

Sarah Conklin

Can I take what I said back?
Whiskey words fighting with sobriety to be heard
one's weapons, truth
the other, envious intoxication.
Because that makes it okay, right?
Tasting the tease of "I'm sorry" runs off my lips
dripping drunk with desperation
I said I'm sorry….
but that wasn't good enough,
because I said it drunk and desperate.

Thou Shalt Not

Ann Gabel

Do I want someone else's man, someone else's woman?
There were days when I thought I must have them, purely
because I shouldn't.
I loved the chase but now I worry,
What would I do if I caught them?

Do I want fancy jewellery and designer clothes,
Hair done at the salon, nails cut and polished?
I bought this – look at this – it cost a lot of money.
I sleep late and I'm happy.

Do I want to travel, have adventures?
Go around the world on a cruise,
Let's do Europe; seven countries in thirty days.
I love my couch, I'll travel from here.

Do I want the best position, the status that goes with it?
Expensive cars and luxury mansions.
I am the boss, the team leader, everyone listens to me.
I have done that, no more thank you,
One ulcer is enough.

Wolf-Pack

Mary Bone

Below the hill from my house,
my friends and I heard a wolf howling.
Envious of the wolf's loud call,
our hope was to howl
like the wolves do.
It was our goal to be a group
other people respected.
We wanted our own special pack.

Piano Envy

Pat Hurley

I wanted to be
Carolyn Mullins
blue-eyed
playing Schubert
softly
blonde ringlets whispering
across my forehead
delicate fingers
close-clipped nails
Schubert/Sherbet
music in pastels.

I wanted to be
my mother
green-eyed
playing water music
running tiny waves along the
keyboard
creating my own Orangerie of
Monet paintings
as I swayed back and forth
on the upright in our
living room.

I wanted to be
Diane Summers
bright-eyed
key-pounding tomboy
next door
slightly tone deaf
all giggles
no practice but softball
no cares
no punishments
soon, no lessons.

But no.
I was all
Gypsy rondos
minor chords
played with sturdy elbows
full-on Bohemian
music made for
Dad's Slovak
brown-eyed "Ondo" side.
pronounced like the French "Andeaux"

But sadly less elegant.

Hi-Fiction

Judah Eli

Thoughts all over,
To the silent girl who keeps collapsing,
TV, music,
Movies moving against the deep while
Monumental expectations fizzle—
But all in all you're content to crawl,
You fall asleep,
Moving, nothing more soothing than being able to run my
fingers against the grooves of your exoskeleton,
God-skeleton,
Godskin,
The hair that made you spin, begin
With images on the fringe—
Hair fringe, lightly-tinged brunette against forehead: godfringe.
When all the lights become prismatic,
The ecstasy ecstatic and cyclical abuse-cycles automatic,
Things feel... kinda static,
Envy on the sun collapse celestial sphincter open when the
statues speak.
Drown out leather couches in the name of expectations,
Bodies without clothes on, undressed to impress in the name of
guilt and frustration,

Chronic lack of patience,
Chthonic haircut thing you'd once expected from others,
What had you expected?
Where are all the others?
Somewhere in a friendless, hypersomniac place
The name of the Underground Sweetheart Machine becomes
Cassiopeia:
The drain hair princess who breaks the magic of all my
chemical parts.
Your nails on the phonescreen,
Tapping text-to-type tits of the Messenger deity as I pray for
extra fingertips,
Emoji runes of digital stone
Crushing me based Facebook god
On www.thigh-highs-and-high-fives.com,
Don't look it up.
When I say I'm a simple bean, or that all women are queens
I'm not trying to make myself into some living, breathing
meme,
All that biscuit-cream between the
Words I say, I genuinely really mean.
Sometimes at night I listen on for footsteps out the window,
Eroding the meaning of home where the implied safety of
Four walls and adobe slats collapses
In a four-point erasure our forebears foreboded,
Forebrain fear of everything that comes before,
The jawless fish walks out the sea and
Wait for it—
Face hits the floor.

Shadowy figures etched in red and black texta,
Texting eyeless ascii art faces in the eyelight, highlighting anxiety in neatly-packaged, ezi-swallowed parts,
Partly obscured, in part by limelight parting lifelike reflections of insincere delight,
But the parts never follow.
Places, lifelines trace faces shivering in the stasis,
Rough social outlines become the blueprints of society,
Afterthoughts to guidelines,
Afterglows sidelines,
Guides in the darklight shining
Black inside the bluelight
I really enjoyed Christian Bale's performance as Batman in
'The Dark Knight'
My thoughts all over,
Find each other quietly.
Change
Colour:
Deliberate distance maintained, scooch a lil closer,
Uh-oh, moment of overwhelming shame,
And you can't help but blame yourself,
Cause you gotta blame something, right?
And every time's the same.
Hair tied in tired pigtails,
I mean, sleep-cycle fees become higher when you leave,
But I'm a liar.
Neglecting basic self-care,
Cutting my hair and
Getting higher,

Standing upright, but airtight on the inside,
Caffeine-high itchy arms but on the inside,
And when I was a kid I didn't even notice **B-P-D** spelt out in alphabet soup,
Or have to jump through mental hoops to explain that—
Sometimes—
A disease isn't always physical,
And sometimes,
Telling someone to "get over it"
Is like the biggest middle-finger to the face
As an insurmountable synonym of
"Fuck you for even trying."
And I have to be honest,
Some days I feel like a motherfucking superstar,
Not all days, but some days,
Because it's **OK** to not be **OK**,
And maybe along the way you'll see best friends resent you for mistaken judgements of intent,
Or old wounds fold over with scar tissue, it's tense,
And maybe detachment is the only way to stay alive sometimes
But sometime, you will find a way of coping,
Because mental wellness is like turning off spell-check in Word,
Sometimes there's nothing wrong with everything you type being underlined in red.

Masquerade

Eileen M. O'Reilly

I envy those who write with ease
Poetic words destined to please
And somehow manage to enclose
A hidden message in their prose
Romantic words which speak of love
Or zealous prayers to gods above
Those who forge words of inspiration
Garner much praise and admiration

How envious am I of those who write
To draw attention to another's plight
Each word is as a single tiny seed
That sparks some deep intrinsic need
To scrutinise its effect on all my senses
Even as it claws at my defences
Words provoke such raw emotions
Change old ideas for brand-new notions

I envy most that sassy writing style
Guaranteed to raise a cheeky smile
Which helps me forget my woes and cares
As happiness momentarily flares
However long the respite lasts
For that brief time I removed the mask
The public face that says I'm fine
Revealed my true self line by poignant line

Envy, It's Not …

R Scott Sexton

37 below—walking into a house—having your glasses fog up so fast you can't see to close the door.

Envy is not
Contemplating the cat's motionless stare through the frosted window at the chickadee foraging at minus 28—scrabbling—remembering—desperate attempt to stay alive.

Envy isn't
Negative 53 Fahrenheit—your frozen breath coagulating on your beard—eyelashes—so thick you can't open your mouth in awe—can barely see the undulating auroral (mostly green with tints of pink—shadows of red), oval pulsating above in an otherwise black sky dominated by so, so many stars—uncountable—interminable—unknown hours away from any scintilla of civilization—isolated—alone.

Envy can't be
Removing your Refrigiwear snowsuit—tying it to your pack—so you won't "break into a sweat", which will kill you at 49 below when you are hours from the road—the warmth—walk three plus miles into the bush, black spruce, Dwarf Birch—cut

survey brush lines—new section of Dalton Highway—so trucks can access the oil fields easier.

Envy cannot be
Ripping your mittens and glove liners off—pressing your bare hands against your cheek—forehead—nose—turning the white flesh—the starting to freeze—to frostbite—flesh—into a facsimile of its former flexible skin.

Envy, It's not
Chartering a bush plane into some lonesome section of roadway just south of the Brooks Range in order to locate a tourist checkpoint area—somebody will build a structure—turn people around—prevent access—Listening to wolves howl from the mountain—getting closer with their call and response—then even closer—still closer—as the already too short day turns into too long dark.

No

Envy is
sitting at an old, oak, rolltop desk—a blank piece of paper—a fountain pen, my favorite writing instrument—Reminiscing—Writing poems.

Who Envies Who?

Carolyn Cordon

Those gorgeous women who totter on heels,
I don't envy them
A trip and a fall, blood isn't so sexy!
I'll stick with my flats & always stay standing.

Those skinny minnies missing their meals,
I don't envy them
Nothing beats a big healthy chow down.
Nutritious is better, that's my understanding!

Those big-time business bitches, dressed for success,
I don't envy them
I have enough, with no need for greed,
the corporate life would be too demanding.

Those private school princesses, so-called activists,
I don't envy them
They're in it for glory, not to give help –
& copy ideas from Social Science reading.

Those teenaged sporting heroines, winning their gold,
I don't envy them
Good genes & hard work, I'd rather rest –
once the body breaks down, it can get degrading.

Those blonde haired beauties, with expensive smiles,
I don't envy them
Skin deep beauty, that won't last
No-one will love them, once their beauty is fading.

Those back to gym yummy mummies, no time to rest,
I don't envy them
Nothing beats loving your very own child
Plenty of hugs & love, with no loveless scolding.

Those brilliant chefs, producing restaurant-level home meals,
I don't envy them
Eventually they'll tire of it, and cook bangers and mash,
Bored and ignored is the path where they're heading.

We all have our ways to get through our lives
& honesty & reality may predict who survives
My life's a simple one, friends who love me, family too –
My answer is clear, on "Who envies who?!"

Child of Comparison

Stephen Seabridge

I get out of bed and stare into the mirror, and I compare   I watch a tea stew out its redness and I compare   I watch the man in the opposite apartment building strip down to shower and I compare   I watch him with the towel, his torso absent of fat, and I compare mine to his, and I imagine what it would be like to wear the chest of another that is not your own   I get into the car in summer wear, bright blue chinos cut off at the knees, the blond hairs of my legs like a coat of gold in the morning, and I compare   compare these legs I have now to the ones before, the thinner, the lither, those that ran for miles and miles and more   I see the woman running through the park, across the frost, her arms bare to the cold and I compare my arms to hers, these limbs lined with silver where the skin was stretched too far   I see the man at the bus stop with his hair thrown back in a quiff, laissez faire, his cheekbones pale like the arches of an amphitheatre, and his long fingers ready for the touch of a piano, and I compare   I go to work at the University and there are signs everywhere: compare, compare, compare written in dead languages, and there is the smoke of cigarettes blending together without comparison, and the younger bodies of others beyond comparison   I hear an American accent, musical tongues, and I compare   compare it to the dryness of my own dialect, compare that to what others say about it, that it might be quaint in the right microphone

I read and compare   I imagine the poet sat in their spot and I compare, and I wonder if they compare too   I hope they compare too   I sit with envy on the internet, in books, I think of those people styled as my rivals and I compare   I eat and compare that food to the bowl of my empty stomach   I stare out of the office window and compare the reflection of my own face to that face the others will see looking out   I think of my own naked body and compare it to my thoughts of it   I look at its reflection when I get home and compare   I think of its previous self and compare   I compare this vehicle to its predecessor, those layers of the body that were absent before, I compare until my bones collect their envies in currencies of dust, until my skin is no longer skin   more a constellation of its own doubts

A.I. VI

Gary Beck

Someday
the electronic home
will be run by A.I.
When you get home
you'll say hello to your door
and it'll let you in.
The robo-server
will take your hat and coat,
bring a drink to your chair,
A.I. will tell you
the articles of interest
in your newspaper,
tv shows on that evening.
All is serene
unless you want to discuss something,
then the know-it-all
aggravates you again
with its smug complacency.
You already gave up chess
because it always beats you.

It knows everything
on the internet
including editorial opinions
so you can't win an argument
because it knows everything.
Yes. The A.I. makes life easy,
but sometimes
I'd like to shut it off
for a little while,
just to be alone again.

Sex Appeal

Steven Deutsch

From his early teens
my fast friend Tom
was fluent in woman.
His at-ease-ness
with the fair sex
was so at odds
with my slight
experience,
I suspected
a pact with Lucifer

I hung around,
hoped that one or more
budding damsel
might tire of Tom
and find my
tight-lipped stammer
and pimpled brows
appealing—
but never
a nibble.

Secretly,
I wished Tom rickets.
I wished him a misstep
on the subway platform
as the 7th Avenue Express
roared through.
I wished that Zeus
would bolt his too easy
heart and leave
him to smolder
in the schoolyard.

Success Story

Edward O'Dwyer

I've been thinking of developing a serious drug addiction,
of struggling with it, then overcoming it,
and then, finally, making something of myself.

I've noticed how people these days
are always talking about how great
those who beat their drug addictions are,
but because I've never had one,
nobody ever talks about me that way.
I notice nobody ever seems to tell anyone
they're great for not having developed a drug addiction.

Some people I grew up with are well in the process.
They are sitting against public bins all day long, begging,
looking like they're not too long for this world.
I'm jealous when I see them there,
rattling loose change in takeaway coffee cups.
I understand that in no time at all
people might be talking about how great they are.

So I guess I will have to go buy some heroin down an alley,
or wherever it is you go these days to buy heroin,
then take it one step at a time, no shortcuts.

Before I know it that dark time in my life
will be in the past, and I'll be firmly
in that bright future of everyone talking about
how great I am to have survived it, and to have turned
my life around and into such a success story.

Prose | Fiction

89	No more Wonderland	*Sue Dawes*
91	Brief Encounter with a Giant Hamburger in the Snow	
	Robert Scotellaro	
93	Different Notes for Different Folks	*Peter Lingard*
95	The Devil's Grandmother	*Beate Sigriddaughter*
96	Kunzman's Rival	*Larry Lefkowitz*
100	Sisters	*Phillis Ideal*
103	The Darkness in Desire	*Monica Fernandez*
105	The Best Grilled Chicken in the World	
	Mike Lewis-Beck	
107	Flight	*Nan Wigington*
109	The Bridesmaid's Speech	*Peter Michal*
113	Someone Like You	*Ebony L. Morman*
116	Obliterated by the Light	*Nod Ghosh*
120	The Question	*Carl Chapman*
123	Fred's Party	*Helen Chambers*
125	Getting There	*Aaron Retz*
127	Pageant	*Steve Carr*
130	Plaything	*Warren Paul Glover*
133	Envy's Spawn	*Reine Marais*
137	The Pain of Beauty	*Mir-Yashar Seyedbagheri*
140	Dumped	*Stephen V. Ramey*
144	The View	*Melisa Quigley*
146	The Return of Red Ledbetter Episode 6	*JP Lundstrom*
149	Eat Pray Envy	*Miriam Mitchell-Bennett*

150	The Training Bra	*Paul Beckman*
152	The Author	*Eddy Knight*
155	Dragons	*Claire Hart*
160	Seedlings of Night	*Bruce Lader*
162	Late Afternoon Delight	*Jackie Davis Martin*
165	Crime of Envy	*Tom Fegan*
168	Green with	*Alison Theresa Gibson*
172	A Writer's Napkin	*Christine Johnson*
175	The Recent History of the Sánchez Family Tragedies: Part VI	*Guilie Castillo Oriard*
179	Jack Beyond the Grave	*Ruth Z. Deming*
182	Who Wears the Pants?	*Jo Hocking*
186	The Bright Man	*E. M. Stormo*
188	Dives	*John Kujawski*
191	NV Road	*Pat O'Connor*
194	The Absent Guest	*Jan McCarthy*
197	Will Take PayPal	*Damian Dressick*
201	Not That Clever	*Alice Little*
205	Janikowski's Solution	*Jim Bell*
209	The Envious Comic	*M Pauseman*
212	Charlie's Girls	*Chloe Timms*
216	Under Her Bed	*Pamela Painter*
219	Venus Envy	*Tim Thompson*
224	The Key	*Michael Webb*
228	Window	*Dan Spencer*

No more Wonderland

Sue Dawes

I hated them the second they were born. Twice as cute: tweedle dumb and tweedle dumber.

'One for each of us,' Mum said to Dad, lifting them up. 'Look at your gorgeous brothers.'

I stood in the corner, shrinking. I didn't even blink.

They got double the love and two-fold of toys. My rewards dried up as their shiny, plastic world expanded.

Mum never once called them unique or different.

Then my parents discovered a flaw but it only made them love my brothers harder.

'Chill,' Dad said, as Mum checked the ingredients on every jar of rainbow coloured food with a magnifying glass. 'No one puts peanuts in baby food.'

The twins reacted differently. I thought they'd be identical.

One puffed up like an overblown balloon, his puckered baby skin almost translucent. The other turned puce and shook like a stammer that can't work its way out of your mouth.

'How could that happen?' Mum asked the Ambulance driver. 'We're so careful.'

'Babies put everything in their mouths, you shouldn't blame yourselves,' the driver said. 'They'll be home soon enough.'

'You okay Alice?' Mum asked me, turning at the ambulance door, before leaving.

I put on my sad face, adjusted my hairband and gave the boys a kiss goodbye, one each, pressing my mouth hard against their skin.

It was hard not to grin but then they'd see the peanuts stuck between my teeth.

Brief Encounter with a Giant Hamburger in the Snow

Robert Scotellaro

He told her he wanted a life that was more like ejecting from a jet plane than getting up from a saggy couch. But he ran out of jets and now the latter prevailed. He was wearing a giant hamburger suit, and said inside it beat the heart of a poet. They stood outside a chain restaurant and smoked cigarettes. It had started to snow and he told her how he once serenaded a girlfriend in fifteen-degree weather below her window with a boom box held over his head.

He told her how he'd like to open up a junkyard someday. "Rusty gold," he said. He told her sometimes he read the Periodic Table of the Elements aloud, just to hear the elegant sounds of those words. He told her how the ancient Egyptians used to think bats had perfect eyesight because of the bugs they snatched out of the air. That they believed a drop of bat blood in each eye could cure blindness.

He said, "So much for assumptions." That he wasn't going to be a giant hamburger or hotdog forever. Said he envied those who glided through life without a care. He said, "Hey, give me your number and maybe we could, you know…"

She said, "Sure," and wrote some numbers she made up on the back of one of the flyers he was handing out.

"Okay," she said.

"Okay," he said.

Then, "Damn," under his breath as he watched her cross the street and vanish into a crowd. "Now ain't she something."

A small dog lifted a leg and added some yellow to a white patch that was gathering. A few flakes landed on some of the rubber ketchup, lettuce, and tomatoes surrounding him, and he didn't mind the cold or the wind one bit. It was a beautiful day.

Different Notes for Different Folks

Peter Lingard

I Like Girls Who Drink Beer keeps repeating like there was too much garlic in the bass when whoever wrote it. Preparing dinner doesn't take enough brainpower to banish the song. Think of something. Wonderful Katherine, who comes from a different background with differing social priorities. I'd walked into a Melbourne hotel bar one night where she was drinking with a couple of suits. I felt envious of the suits, wondering which one would end up with her. It didn't take long to realise the suits were too in touch with their effeminate sides and she'd be better off with me. Katherine had said, as I was drinking alone I should join them. She and I ended up in the same place with the same intentions, and I found she was a perfect fit.

She owns a dress and swimwear shop that bears the name Kitty, and I have a small construction company. She's a member of a country club where she meets her social set, gossips, drinks, and dines. I told her a country club should play country music and have line dancing and boot scootin' boogies every Saturday night. She laughed when I said that. The closest it gets is in the ballroom once a year for the Last Night of The Proms, which, I must admit, isn't that bad. Our tastes in clothes are miles apart. She's a fashionista and I like checkered shirts, faded jeans, and expensive boots. She drives a Merc and I like my HiLux. We have loud fights and louder recoveries. I'm being dishonest. I dress up for special occasions when I drink wine instead of beer. We'll drive two hours for a good feed, always in the Merc as she wouldn't be seen dead in what she calls 'my rusty wreck', despite it being relatively new. She lets me drive her precious wheels because, she says, 'what man wants to be seen driven around by a woman', but in reality because she can then swig two-thirds of whatever plonk we purchase.

Sometimes we enjoy a few drops of Talisker together. We pass books to each other, and prefer Trump tweets to the Comedy Channel. We go to just about every theatrical production staged in Melbourne. We watch sports together; cricket, netball, the Melbourne Storm and I've even embedded in her a love for my favourite football team, Manchester City.

It's been a couple of years now, and we'll be ending soon. The fun is less spontaneous; more serious. Having to make appointments to have sex (which was our 'raison d'etre') between a day's work and an evening's fashion show is a pain. We've got what we wanted from the relationship, both having previously been brutalised by hostile divorces, and we've given each other the confidence to look for something more substantial with someone else.

I Like Girls Who Drink Beer. It's still in my head! I put down the peeler, turn on the radio, and select the station that airs golden oldies. *Itsy Bitsy Teeny Weeny Yellow Polka Dot Bikini.* That'll do. I loudly noise the unknown words and slide on the tiled floor in my socks. Kitty's back. I hear the door clunk and then her voice shouting over the music. 'We obviously connect on more than one level, Guy. Turn around and take a look what I stole from my stock.' She opened wide her coat. 'It doesn't have polka dots but I think it does the job. What do you reckon?'

The Devil's Grandmother

Beate Sigriddaughter

All the world's a stage

William Shakespeare

Oh, she was lovely, dainty, a tiny nose, a rosebud mouth. Her mother bought her every advantage, voice lessons, dance lessons, figure skating lessons, and she was a star on every stage. For me funds were limited to piano. I got the better grades in school, but how I envied her perpetual stardom. One year we shared a stage. She was the princess of course, I merely a forest fairy, helping the hero prevail in his quest for her exquisite hand. On the black and white cast photo the two of us smile flanking the hero and the devil in the front row. Slightly behind me, in an apron and with horns—they were red I recall—the devil's grandmother with a sour expression.

My new slogan, fifty-some years later: At least I didn't have to play the devil's grandmother.

Kunzman's Rival

Larry Lefkowitz

As I climbed the stairs to Victoria's apartment, I passed a man descending who looked familiar. In profile, he looked like a Roman emperor. His black hair was swept back behind large ears, showing a high forehead and a forceful, prominent nose. His features reflected a certain old-world vanity and charm. How different from Lieberman, Victoria's late husband.

He was a well-known Jerusalem gallery owner-cum-painter, Maximilian Krim by name. Krim, like his near-named, Benya Krik, the Jewish gangster "King" of Isaac Babel's *Odessa* stories, was a fabulous dresser. If Krik preferred an orange suit and a diamond bracelet, Krim went in for the dark striped suits of a Mafioso don, often garnished with a red rose in the lapel and, somewhat incongruously, contrasted by bedazzling brightly colored shirts with the initials of his name emblazoning the pocket. The shirts specifically designed for him (according to his claim) or (according to rumor) the initials skillfully sewn on by a paramour-painter in return for exhibiting her paintings free of charge in his gallery. His sartorial appearance was rounded off by his full throat supporting not a tie, but a huge gold (or gold-plated) necklace, which gave him the appearance of a Lord Mayor of London risen from Cockney ranks.

This description may be tendentious on my part (though Lieberman, the eminent literary critic and my late employer, called him "the Jewish Narcissus"), since I was an indifferent dresser, although I strove to improve the situation to please Victoria, whom I was pursuing. Krim was a brash, garrulous man who took far more words than necessary to tell more than he knew (pooh-poohed by Lieberman as his "torrential eloquence").

Thick in the shoulders and legs, Krim suited Lieberman's description that he "would make a good support for an acrobatic troupe's pyramid." A quality which came in handy when, at a cocktail party or paintings exhibition, he spied a beautiful woman (Lieberman maintained that Krim "had a prejudice against women who were not beautiful") talking to a man; he would plant his mass in front of the latter, blocking him out of the conversation, and begin subjecting the woman to his verbal charm. He was known for unsheathing the expression, delivered in a baritone voice, "Grand passions are as rare as masterpieces," which I knew he stole from Balzac. I took little comfort from the fact that Krim's masterpieces were rarer than his passions.

Victoria liked to refer to Krim as "my *cher maitre*" – perhaps to needle me. I wondered if Victoria had referred to Krim as her "*cher maitre*" in Lieberman's day as she did in mine. The title conjured up an Old Master painter in smock and beret; Krim was too fashion-conscious for such unprepossessing garb—he would opt for an Edwardian smoking jacket, overly garnished with some Krimian touch. In order to get back at her for using this *nominis umbra*, I would refer to him as her *petit-maitre*, meaning a dandy, a fop, but also an artist of minor importance. She applied to it its literal meaning of 'little master', unaware of its pejorative usage. Once I realized this, I ceased to use the title.

On one occasion, I forget in which context, I forbore not and mocked his latest gimmick of putting a bit of actual sand in his paintings of the desert, or coral in his beach epics.

"Authenticity!" thundered Victoria. "Trompe l'oeil."

"Trompe la poche," I countered.

On a second occasion, I said about Krim, "Every single sentence of his oozes artifice and pose. Not to speak of his paintings which exemplify Warhol's statement that art is 'what you can get away with.'"

Victoria raised an eyebrow – actually, both eyebrows – Victoria did nothing in halves. "You're jealous of him because he knows more about paintings than you do."

"Never, never, never, never, never," I exclaimed, borrowing from King Lear.

"Don't exaggerate, Kunzman. Going to a gallery with Krim is like seeing with four eyes, my two and his two. "

When I said to Victoria that in my opinion Krim was a failure as a painter and a person, Victoria jumped to his defense. "Your problem is that you feel yourself consistently underappreciated."

"Me!"

"You!"

So much for pronoun discourse. And after Victoria had thus raised her cudgels against me, she took them up to defend Krim by quoting the poor besmirched (drawing herself up in her Aida pose and with a voice to match): "In our life there is a single color, as on an artist's palette, which provides the meaning of life and art. It is the color of love." Unfortunately, its source didn't come to me until two days later (found in a book of quotations under "Love") – Marc Chagall. When I pointed it out to Victoria, she replied, "Are you still going on about Krim?" Vanquished, but at least she called him "Krim" and not "my *cher maitre*." When I then threw out my final word on the subject, hinting at Krim's dalliances, Victoria replied that he was a "*homme à femmes*." She made it sound like a compliment. I wanted to put her *homme à femmes hors d'usage*, but

I was ill-equipped to compete with his repertoire of hand-kissing, bowing, fussing over, flowers, and raised-glass toasting. I settled for mumbling "*'homme d'affaires'* – romantic affairs."

"Why do you always focus on peccadillos?"

"*Peccadillos!*"

"Trifles."

Silence.

"You're a prude. P-R-U-D-E."

"Thanks for spelling it out."

"At least Krim is never sullen."

This I took as a dig at yours truly. The word she had used disturbed me. 'Moody', 'glum', 'sulky', even 'morose', I could live with. Not 'sullen'.

Victoria shook her head in her hair-fluffing gesture of dismissal of my criticism of Krim. "He is, when not in his debonair, courtly mood, an oppressive man, insufferable, unpleasant to be with. But he is an artist. You don't understand, Kunzman, the art world stresses the cult of the personality." I couldn't help thinking that this might explain her attraction to Lieberman! At the same time, I felt insulted – that I didn't measure up in her eyes, lacking in sufficient caliber. Victoria's reluctance to break off with Krim was consistent with her ability, when necessary, to slam a door without quite closing it. And Krim was second to no one in his ability to get a foot in the door.

And more than a foot in Victoria's door, I was having trouble getting a toehold.

Sisters

Phillis Ideal

Four little girls raced up the stairs to the second-floor bedroom to claim their favorite ensemble from the dress-up trunk. Each step took them farther away from the clinking cocktail glasses and raucous laughter of the adults, assembled in the large living room on the ground floor. The turn of the century house's spacious rooms, high ceilings, and cushioned window seats were the perfect setting to play "Little Women," based on Louisa May Alcott's novel and the 1949 movie.

They had seen the movie countless times and knew the story by heart but their script was made up, and the clothing their mothers had donated was reconfigured to adorn the character they had chosen to play. Jo was tailored, Amy was frivolous with ribbons and bows, Meg was plain and sensible; and Beth, who was ill and had no costume changes, wore the same nightgown throughout the dress-up session.

Each time they climbed to the top of the steps, they encountered a large framed photograph of the sisters who lived in the house. It was a textbook example of sibling rivalry: Morgan, who was seven, could not tolerate four-year-old Abby, who wanted to be included and copy her older sister. The photograph captured Morgan glowering down at Abby, her eyes narrowed, her young brow wrinkled, and a smirk pulled at one corner of her mouth. She wanted her little sister to vanish and nothing of her to ever be found. Better yet, she wished she had never been born. She cut her sister out of snapshots leaving gaping holes that lassoed the depth of her envy. In contrast, Abby was grinning ear-to-ear, always obedient when asked for a big smile.

Morgan, who fiercely played Meg, the eldest sister in "Little Women," rearranged the original story in which Beth dies of scarlet fever near the end of the second half of the book. She commanded that Beth die immediately, almost at the beginning of the play session, to get rid of Abby, who was always assigned the role of the sick Beth.

"Beth, you are dead," she would trumpet, "and no longer with us. So leave."

Two patches of bright anger bloomed on Abby's cheeks, a soggy stream of tears drowned her face, and sobs shook her small body. She wadded up her gown so she would not trip and stumbled toward the stairs, once again, to report to her mother that she had not been allowed to play. The other girls were uncomfortable with this bullying but dodged confronting Morgan, counting on an adult to handle this recurring situation. Morgan was the ringleader and the glue that grounded the story. If the other two girls had refused to play according to Morgan's rules, they feared the dress-up game would break up, and they would lose something that they might never get back: the path of who they could become. The girls were selfishly intent on inhabiting their chosen role models and speaking through their favorite character.

Abby began to howl as she reached the living room filled with half-drunk adults. Her grandmother picked her up and said, "I have just the answer. You and I will make some wonderful sugar cookies. You can stir the mixture and lick the bowl and help me cut out different shapes. These cookies will be just for you, and we will keep them in this cookie jar in the pantry. You will not have to share them with anyone."

Morgan's envy reached fever pitch when she saw the pleasure that making cookies afforded her little sister. She watched her swirling the flour, sugar, and butter in a large bowl with a tasting spoon to lick as she popped the cookie sheet in the oven; and had a short wait to again feel sugar's soothing effects.

One night when Abby was fast asleep, Morgan changed out the sugar for salt, and eagerly awaited the next time that Abby made cookies and had her first bite.

The Darkness in Desire

Monica Fernandez

The stage of the Wonderland Nightclub is divided by a plexiglass wall separating stage left and stage right.

Stage Left: An alleyway outside. It's cold. A fire burns in the barrel of an empty oil can. Homeless vagabonds in rags are huddled around it for warmth.

Stage Right: A burlesque show. Scantily clad women performing sultry dances. A normal show at Wonderland.

Every so often, one of the Rags would throw a dirty look at those in the Riches. The audio in the club is also separated – mono instead of stereo, half and half, split right down the middle. Those on the left hear the crackling of the fire, the whirr of chilly wind, the distant sounds of a party next door. Those on the right hear the chatter of the party, the laughter and the upbeat music the girls are dancing to.

Waiters stroll through the right half of the audience, providing complimentary drinks.

Those on the left get nothing.

Some of the Rags on stage grow desperate. They knock on the glass, then pound on it, yelling for attention. No one in the club can hear them. No one even bothers to look. The dancers continue to perform, leaving the stage, walking through the right half of the audience. They don't look at the left.

The rest of the Rags join in on the banging. The plexiglass threatens to bow. They yell at the audience, trying to get the attention of the dancers, who are too busy to hear them. A riot erupts against the glass. Rocks, trash, and eventually the flaming oil can itself are thrown against the wall. Nothing happens.

Eventually the fighting, the yelling, the screaming, dies down. The Rags slide against the glass wall or sink to their knees at the front of the stage, dejected, hopeless, fed up. Tired.

One by one, they realize they'll never get what they want. They'll never make it through the glass.

They'll never have the life, the love, the girl, the body, that's just beyond their reach.

The Rags trail off stage.

Gunshots are heard from the wings, accompanied by flashes of light.

The lights dim. The sound on both sides fades. The dancers return to the stage.

Despondency settles in the audience. This isn't the performance they were expecting, but it's the one they deserve.

The darkness in desire, in envy, isn't jealousy or the actions that stem from it.

The darkest part is what you realize about yourself when you fall into it.

That's a pit you can never recover from.

The Best Grilled Chicken in the World

Mike Lewis-Beck

This morning I breakfasted in a lemon light, an egg yolk light, light the color of a *nata*, delicious custard tart of Lisboa, my home city. It's not just the Lisbon light today, sweet as it is. It's more, because I've come home from my studies in America, in what New Yorkers call 'flyover country.' I'm a painter and a poet, have been studying regionalist painters, did a thesis on Thomas Hart Benton. After breakfast this morning I revisited the historic home of my favorite poet—Pessoa, man of many masks. All day I've been strolling the city, its parks and cobbled streets, pondering the beauty of our blue ceramic tiles and the curiosity of our national bird, a proud rooster with a glorious red comb.

 I couldn't quit thinking about that bird as I sat down early evening to eat the best grilled chicken in the world—at Bonjardim, a local place in the Rossio quarter. I'd eaten here before, many times, knew it was the best. I ordered my standard: half a chicken off the spit, a pile of fries, half bottle of Setúbal white, green olives and goat cheese for starters, all served by a welcoming waiter with a Brazilian wife. We hit it off, both being left-handed, something I saw again when he switched around my place setting. A crowded Saturday night, everyone happy to be out of the sudden rain, elbow to elbow, wiping the aromatic drippings off their faces. That's when I heard it, the familiar accents of American tourists.

"We don't do chicken that way in Kentucky," the jowled man at the next table said to me. Startled from my private homecoming feast, I stopped carving the delicately browned top of a succulent thigh. I nodded, then continued eating, with special attention to a golden French fry, crisped to perfection. My hope was to go on with my selfish reverie, but I recalled my debt to American hospitality. Turning to my fresh acquaintance from Kentucky, I said, in my practiced Midwestern English, "Perhaps you might like our chicken. It's finger-lickin' good."

"You speak English," declared the Kentucky gentleman (from Paducah I overheard), pushing on. "We pan fry it." I looked at him, and raised my glass of wine in his direction. "To your health, kind sir," I said. He tugged at my tablecloth, pointed at my plate. "Another thing. That ain't got gravy. Be better with red-eye."

I took the bait. "Why would you want gravy on grilled chicken?" The diner across from us jumped in. "Grilled-spilled. Fiddle sticks. In Indiana we deep fry. No crunch at all, this greasy stuff." He shoved his platter away, tossed down his napkin, took a serious pull off his beer bottle. Struggling for a recovery, I said: "See you like our beer." The Hoosier responded: "It's OK. Not cold enough though."

The penny dropped. I finally got it. They envied our fine grilled chicken, indeed were drooling for it, but couldn't let go of their own home pride, something I understood well. "Why did you come to Lisbon?" I tentatively asked this gathering community of my new American friends. The Hoosier replied: "Me and the Mrs just love to travel to different places overseas, enjoy how other folks live. Last time did the British Isles."

Flight

Nan Wigington

Alcohol straddled my stomach and beat at my chest as if I had died. She flung my mouth open. No rescue breaths, but something hot and sweet against my teeth. I gasped. She laughed. Hard and sharp like the glass breaking.

Put on shoes, I told myself, *Her shards are everywhere.*

"Wake up," she shouted.

I didn't want to. Why did I have to? She raked her nails across my forehead. I raised my brows, opened my eyes as if this could staunch the wounds. My mouth was frangible crust. Articulation might have shattered the peace of my ragged tongue. I didn't respond.

But my eyes opened. I saw again. The beauty of this mess. Red hair, green eyes, skin sparkling like the night. So many stars. Did the wanting hurt more than the having? Her touch burned, nourished. Horns rose from my hips. An oasis sprung from my thighs.

I put my two cotton arms on her steel shoulders and shoved.

"Off," I commanded. Or did I murmur?

She rolled away giggling.

"Tee-hee," she said. "I can soar, and you can't."

I blinked. A memory of night and flight and skies crept up my throat. Was it a comet or the feathers of her hair that made me so sick? She was the universe's beginning and ending, the weight of wax and the whisper of wings.

I reached for her mouth, her breast.

"I know when to stop," I said, but I was tasting her lips, guzzling the corners of her flesh.

She put her hand on my nipple and pinched.

It hurt.

But you are on top, I told myself.

I moaned. Oh, the lovers she'd had.

You are the best, I told myself.

I moved hard against her.

The pavement beneath me left its scars.

The Bridesmaid's Speech

Peter Michal

The bride and groom were friends of ours, which is to say I barely knew them at all and was, not for the first time, making up the numbers at a social event.

He cried during the exchange of vows and she looked beautiful. Guns N' Roses' *November Rain* played on loop throughout the ceremony, which concluded with a kiss, and yet more crying on the part of the groom, a concreter by trade. Go figure.

And then it was time for photos out in nature, among the vines and apple trees of the hills estate, first with family and close friends, then with the second tier of friends, like us, and then with anyone who was left, like the catering staff and the DJ.

They opened the bar, not too soon, and the reception kicked into gear. Two glasses of Moscato on an empty stomach and the bridesmaid — the older, unmarried sister — was ready for her speech.

'Every waking moment up to now, whether you have been aware of it or not,' she began, addressing the happy couple, 'has been leading to this day, to this occasion, to this very moment, which is the start of not only a new chapter, but a new process, one that will evolve as you age and change in each other's presence, through good times and challenging times, and all the times in between.'

Oh, shit, I thought, standing at the back of the room, sipping from my own glass of disgusting bubbly. This is going to get metaphysical. Fuck it.

'It will evolve as you evolve,' the bridesmaid continued, 'but this process will ultimately see your love for one another toughen to form the hardest substance of all. Not iron. Not chromium steel. Not even diamond will be able to match for strength what your love for one another will become.'

I looked over at The Girl, my partner, the one whose friends these people actually were. 'What about tungsten?' I asked her, under my breath.

She laughed, but then cut it off.

'Tungsten's pretty tough,' I said.

'Shush,' she told me.

'What about cobalt? They make drill bits out of that stuff.'

The bridesmaid read on. 'Forged in the supernova of your coming together, that moment when eye met eye and an explosion of love occurred, the bond you now share with each other is unbreakable.'

'Just like a Toyota HiLux,' I whispered to The Girl.

Again, she sniggered, this time hiding her blushing face behind her hand. Once composed, she stabbed me in the side with an index finger. Second warning.

'Like two newly-born celestial stars,' the bridesmaid went on, and on, 'your lights will burn brightest in the sky, fuelled not by nuclear fusion, but the energy given off by the other.'

I looked around the room at the sea of nodding heads. Either these people did not understand the universal laws of physics, or they too had consumed two glasses of Moscato on an empty stomach. Both, I suspected, given the state of public education and alcohol consumption in this country.

The Girl started sniggering again. I gave her a look. 'Something I didn't say?' I asked.

'I love it,' she laughed behind her hand.

'What?'

'The bridesmaid.'

'What about her?'

'She's jealous of the bride and groom. She's so jealous she's mocking their earnest love for each other. Listen to her.'

I studied the older sister again. Head bowed, she gripped the microphone tightly, knuckles turning to white. Her speech, practiced with wine in hand earlier, did not falter though.

'May your celestial stars burn bright, through the good times,' she said, tracing over familiar ground, 'and the challenging times, and all the mundane times in between…'

'Ha!' The Girl laughed out loud, before quickly covering her mouth with her hand. The groom's Polish mother, seated at the front of the room, turned back to give us the daggers. I felt the redness run down my face.

'For there will be those, undoubtedly,' the bridesmaid intoned, saving our blushes. 'In between the holidays to Bali and Phuket, the new Mazda 3 Mum is going to get you, the kitchen renovations, the new deck and all the happy occasions spent entertaining guests on it, there will be mundane days spent under the one roof together, in that nicely-landscaped three-bedroom house in the western suburbs, the one with the new Mazda 3 in the driveway…'

The bridesmaid looked up from her speech for the first time. 'You'll love it,' she said with a forced smile. 'You'll love all of it'.

The gathered crowd, having re-entered the Earth's atmosphere, took a moment to realise the speech was finally over. They broke out in applause.

The Girl, next to me, started shaking her head as she clapped along.

'What is it?' I asked her.

'That bitch is so envious, it's hilarious!'
'Really?'
'Oh, yeah.'

I turned back to the bridesmaid. Smiling through gritted teeth, her jaw muscles flexed with sinful thoughts.

Someone Like You

Ebony L. Morman

Malik pulls me closer. Against my better judgement, I don't protest. I am intrigued. All I can think about is his hands around my waist, mine around his neck and our movement as we catch the beat. I hear bass, treble and instruments. No words.

His mouth nears my earlobe. When the two body parts connect, I flinch.

"You having fun?" he questions.

I smile. Why do I feel guilty? It's just one silly dance. No foul. No harm.

He pulls his head back just enough to see my face. My smile disappears. He smiles.

"I'll take your silence as confirmation," he laughs.

We dance, not missing a beat. I smile on the inside. Yes, I should feel guilty.

"Last call!" the bartender yells over the sound system. The warning sends at least twenty people rushing to the bar. We head back to our table.

"What's this all about?" Tariq questions.

"Holding hands, huh?" Leah adds.

We look at our hands. We don't let go.

"How else do you suppose we get through a crowded club?" I spit back.

I feel Malik's touch willing me to calm down.

"Fine," I say as I take a seat next to Tariq. "I wasn't the one who dared us to dance."

Tariq motions for me to sit on his lap. I'm in a trance, watching Malik passionately kiss his girlfriend before taking a seat.

I wish we were back on the dance floor. I try to shake that feeling. It was just a dare, right?

"I'm starving," I say.

"What's new, Jordyn?" Tariq teases.

I don't take the bait.

I take the lead and sit at the bar. Malik sits to my right. Leah grabs the bar stool next to him.

"I'll sit by my girl Leah," Tariq says. "I'm feeling tension from that side."

I roll my eyes. Malik laughs.

"The usual," we say to the waiter.

Diner food after the club is tradition. Tonight, I need comfort food.

I glance down the bar. Malik is still looking at the menu. Leah and Tariq are glued to her cell phone, probably filtering a selfie and thinking of a groundbreaking caption.

I zero in on Tariq. I look at him like I have so many times before tonight. I no longer see the man I fell in love with freshman year. I yearn for something real.

It is 2:00 a.m. when we kiss our men good-bye. I am exhausted.

"Did you enjoy yourself?" Leah asks.

She pulls off her shoes one by one and tosses them near the front door. I pick them up and place them neatly next to mine.

"Don't forget my spoon, J!" Leah demands.

I try to recount the many date nights followed by ice cream and recaps. Another tradition.

"I did," I reply making my way to the couch.

"That's vague," Leah says, dipping her spoon into the ice cream.

"Did you?" I question.

"I did," Leah replies.

There is an unusual moment of silence between two friends.

"I think you and Malik would make a great couple," Leah fills the silence. "He's too soft for me. I know I need someone to take con-"

"Control?" I finish her sentence.

"Yup," Leah says.

"Someone like Riq?" I hesitate.

"Someone like Riq," Leah repeats. The thought resonates.

"Yea, someone like Tariq," we say in unison.

Obliterated by the Light

Nod Ghosh

After Shelley left – she took the next northbound flight – Pascal and I realised our relationship had curdled and died.

Nothing was discussed. No accusations. No tears, no declarations.

We said nothing about how my best friend had destroyed our relationship.

I didn't see Pascal for a month. The pain cut me in two.

A month later, he begged me to go back to him.

"No." I turned away from him. "Never."

"Please, Hannah." Pascal cried into a handkerchief. He didn't cry easily.

I walked away.

I went back north for the final year of college. I didn't see Shelley. She didn't go to the feminist socialist meetings anymore. I went along hoping she'd be there, so I could ignore her. I met a bunch of dykes at those meetings. Some liked drinking good coffee almost as much as they liked pussy.

That's how Grace Somers came into my life. Grace had a mouth made from chillies and razor wire. She knew Shelley and didn't have a good word to say about her, though I sensed something complex behind her snide remarks. Like it was the sort of hate that grew out of love.

Grace dropped in one morning for a cuppa. She was exploring my gallery of pictures and paintings while we waited for the kettle to boil.

"When was this taken?" She tapped her finger on a picture of Shelley and me pinned on the board. I'd taken most pictures of her down, but missed one.

"That was in my first year."

"How many years ago?" Grace sipped her Jamaican Blue Mountain. She drank it black.

"Three? Four? She'd just had her tattoo done. We were celebrating."

"The snake tattoo on her ankle?"

"You've seen it?"

"Like, millions of times." Grace ran a hand through her scrunched curls.

"You used to be close, hey?" I ventured.

"Once-upon-a-fuckin'-time."

"Me too. We were best friends," I said, wondering why I hadn't known about Grace. What else had my *best friend* concealed?

"She was jealous of you, wasn't she?" Grace bit into a biscuit.

"Jealous? What have *I* got for Shelley Moon to be jealous of?"

"She just was. You can see resentment in her eyes. Here. Look."

"Bullshit."

"No, see the way she's looking at you. When the two of you are together, you overshadow her. She's obliterated by your light."

"Oh come on. Flattery won't turn me gay."

"Fuck off. Don't fancy you anyway, Hannah. You're too tall. I like my girls petite."

"You fuck off," I said. "Seriously, that's bollocks though." Surely it couldn't be true? I hoped Grace would elaborate anyway. It was a bizarre idea, but I wanted to taste it a little longer, even if it was fantasy. Grace didn't say anything.

"Everyone wanted to be like her back then," I said. "Everyone wanted to be Shelley Moon. I would have died to have sung on stage like her." I gathered some folders for my next lecture. "Anyway, how can you tell what someone's thinking from a photo?"

"It's not just that," Grace said, peeling up the corner of another picture. "She envied you. I know that for a fact. We haven't always been enemies, Shelley and I. Anything but. Though that's a story for another day, or I'll be late. I've got a meeting."

We left my flat together, went in different directions.

After my lecture, I walked through the Union. Shelley was selling tickets for one of her gigs. She was supporting some bigwig, a great opportunity for her. I joined the queue. My heart was thumping like a rotary hammer drill. All I could think about was Pascal. Shelley and Pascal. Yet I tried to come across like I didn't care.

"Hannah!"

If there was any hesitation, any embarrassment on Shelley's part, it lasted less than a second.

"Hi." I opened my purse. "One ticket for Friday." My composure was slipping. My voice wavered.

"Don't be silly, I'll put you on the guest list." She scribbled something on a piece of paper on a clipboard. There was no one else in the queue behind me, so I had no excuse to leave. "There's a party afterwards," she added. "You've got to come." She was stupidly enthusiastic, like a blowfly buzzing around shit. Desperate. "When did you get back?" she asked. "Why didn't you come to see me?"

I wanted to say: *I haven't been to see you, you ignorant bitch, because you shagged my boyfriend right under my nose. Did you think I wouldn't notice?*

What I actually said was, "Sure, I'll see you after the gig." My tongue knotted into a ball and threatened to slide down my throat and gag me. I was on the verge of telling Shelley to screw herself, when someone came up behind me for tickets.

So Shelley and I carried on where we'd left off. The summer was never mentioned. She needed me as much as I needed her. And I did need her. I needed her radiance. I missed her sapphire light, her circle of friends. Shelley moved in circles I wanted to inhabit.

I wasn't going to drop her.

Soon it seemed like Pascal was from a separate universe, like our relationship had never happened.

I'd never seen the guy's colours properly, though I'd believed I knew them. They were the black of diamonds, the cerise of tulips.

Grace was a more complex hue. Blue and sea and pain and that particular shade of green that signifies want.

And what of Shelley? What colour was my friend? Her gilt was corroding and flaking. I could see the snake-browns and ash-greys beneath her glamour.

That year, she shed her skin, and for the first time, I began to see Shelley Moon for what she really was.

I began to see that I'd been obliterated by her black light.

I wasn't going to allow that to happen again.

The Question

Carl Chapman

Michael debated what to say in response to a question that he should have known would eventually arise. He had been dating Wendy for about a month now and the two of them had been gradually moving further into going to bed. So far it hadn't got to that point, but now here it was. Here they were on a couch in her living room with her parents upstairs asleep and the two of them in a hot embrace that he was certain was leading to sex. He'd been down this road enough times to read the signals.

He thought about her question. It was amazing how time could seem to stop, and this was one of those times. A simple *yes* would move things forward into the realm of trust and vulnerability, and once that line was crossed there was no turning back. Michael knew this from his past experiences with women. Once you slept with a woman, the deed was done, and you were committed even if there was an understanding of no commitment. That never happened, no matter how much was stated beforehand.

Just say yes, the voice in his head kept repeating. *She's hot. Don't you want to know what's under those clothes? You've fantasized often enough?*

Yeah, but you don't love her, and you know it, voiced the other side of him.

So, what difference does that make? You've slept with women you didn't love before?

Yeah, but the love was implied, never directly stated before having sex. That's the difference now. If I tell her I love her and have sex with her then I'll be using her, and she'll eventually know that.

So? She wants to have sex now. She's ready. All she wants is a reason to do it. Just give her the reason and move on.

I can't do that.

You know what will happen if you don't say yes, you'll be tossed out of the house faster than a guy selling door to door – if they even do that anymore.

Sensing hesitation, Wendy kissed him again, and he reciprocated, hoping the kiss would suffice as the answer. One look into her eyes told him that it wouldn't. It was time to decide, yes or no?

Don't say it, came the voice. *Please, God, don't say it. Think of the Mustang!*

Wendy's father had bought her a '71 Mach 1 Mustang for her birthday, which she let Michael drive on their dates. He figured she allowed him to drive it because she didn't want to ride in his old faded green Plymouth Fury, and it also probably looked weird to her to be driving her male date around.

Michael hadn't thought about the Mustang, which he enjoyed speeding around in and acting cool with a beautiful girl alongside him. He mostly liked the look of envy other guys gave him when they drove together by a crowd. Even the girls checked him out. Yeah, there was nothing like driving money on wheels to appeal to a hot girl or to make a lesser man jealous. Now the decision had just become a tad more difficult because the appearance of his manhood was at stake.

With one more kiss, he knew the decision had to be made. He could sense the impatience in her persistence.

He made his decision, and that inner voice responded quickly. *Get ready to leave.*

"Wendy, I like you a lot, but I'm not ready to make that leap yet. I don't think we've had enough time for me to go that far. I don't want to say yes just to be able to go farther with this. I hope you understand."

Pulling away from him, with a tear at the corner of her left eye, she quickly said, "I think you better go."

"Wendy—"

"Just leave."

With that, Michael quickly picked up his coat, closed the door behind him and silently climbed into his Plymouth Fury.

His whole drive back home, the inner voice kept saying, *I told you so*. But the other side of him was pleased with himself. He hadn't taken advantage. He'd done the right thing. Maybe later she'd be grateful for his honesty, but then again, maybe she wanted him to lie. Maybe she'd wanted him to tell her what she wanted to hear and deal with the consequences later. Sometimes a lie was better than the truth, but as for him, the truth felt pretty good right now, although he was going to miss that Mustang and the looks of envy from all the guys who watched him behind the wheel.

Fred's Party

Helen Chambers

From: Molls
To: Nell, Fi, Annie, Fred, Luce +36 others

Thursday

SUMMER PIMM'S PARTY at ours, Saturday evening, standard arrangements!
Partners welcome!

Mollie and Jack xxx

From: Fred
To: Mollie, Jack, Nell, Fi, Annie + 36 others

Sunday

Wonderful Molls (and the admirable Jack),
Thanks so much for a **BRILLIANT** party in your beautiful home: no wonder you've had shots taken by the glossies. Haven't enjoyed myself so much in ages. You looked gorgeous, darling – best-dressed woman there without a doubt. Mind you, not much competition – Hannah doing the Mexican Wave five minutes after everyone else – and what was that kaftan-thing she wore?! Laugh? I nearly died every time I caught your eye. Ed looked pretty embarrassed by her. And

Lucy and Annie in those tawdry identical dresses, which no ordinary mortal could actually afford, and Lucy – 'curvy,' isn't she? – saying it was coincidental. Annie's mouth pursed into a cat's arse all evening (naturally or because of fillers?). Still spluttering when I think about it all! That yawn-inducing Jo-Jo droning on about the many and varied celebs she mixes with at her fat-busting class. Lucy could try it, she seemed impressed… And then when Nell threw her drink in Fi's ear and Fi screamed about needing an ambulance! Classic! Your coupled-up friends are priceless, my darling.

Hope you and Jack are still speaking after you and Ed sloped off together… naughty girl! You're a dark horse!

Fred xx

From: Molls
To: Fred

Sunday

Fred – you 'replied all' you faithless, stupid git.

M

From: Fred
To: Mollie, Jack, Nell, Fi, Annie, Jo-Jo + 36 others

Yesterday 09.15

Darlings – only joking, my dears! I would never really mean such horrid things about people so important to me. It didn't mean anything at all. Forgive me my thoughtless joke!

Your friend, Fred

Getting There

Aaron Retz

I went to a meditation joint this morning, upstairs from the community centre near the shops. I wandered in feeling confused and anxious and met this skinny old (sixtyish?) guy named Pat, who takes some of the classes. He was friendly, but also pretty intense. He's got these slightly creepy smoke-coloured eyes—real penetrating. He wanted to know why I was there.

So I just blurted out how me and Amy are soul mates, and how she simply ended contact for her own mysterious reasons. How I stopped going to work and drank myself stupid for a week and a half. How every song on the radio is about love, how books and movies are pretty much the same, how the whole world feels like a melancholy theatre.

I told Pat how yesterday I saw myself in the mirror and got a hell of a shock—I saw a corpse, and felt utterly dead inside.

Pat told me it's normal to feel like crap when your heart is broken because it's how we're all taught to respond. But just because it's normal to flip out when someone rejects you, it doesn't mean you *have* to. He gave me a little book about 'non-attachment' (said I could keep it—didn't even ask for any money) and told me to come back later that day for the mindfulness meditation class.

I've been curious about meditation for a while but was never quite sure why. Now I know. Because life sucks and I need to harden up. Well, actually, it's not really about hardening up. Take Pat. He's as soft as they come.

During the class Pat spoke about sitting still, focusing on the breath, and just allowing any thoughts we had to come and go. And not getting annoyed with the thoughts. The point is to not hang onto or judge them. I couldn't stop thinking about Amy, of course, but Pat would gently remind me (and the other two people there) to soften our attitude toward any thoughts that entered our mind.

I've got to admit, it actually *almost* worked! After about twenty minutes of having Amy zooming around in my head, I let it go, like I was saying 'goodbye' and 'it's okay' at the same time. It was (almost?) an acceptance of this shitty situation I'm in. At this point I found my eyes swelling with silent tears.

Afterwards I had a cup of green tea with Pat in a little kitchen behind the activity room. Pat's married without kids. He met his wife in high school but they didn't get together until they were both late-thirties. He said they decided to be together after being good friends for so long and comfortable in their own skin. It was obvious that Pat was painting a different picture to the intense (to the point of *totally insane*) kind of love that I'd expressed for Amy earlier that morning.

I said, I know this is all moving a bit fast, but will you be my guru? I told him I'm sick of being constantly tossed around by my emotions and that I *really* want the chilled out vibe he's got. My mind had already started churning over the idea of trying to do life without Amy.

Pat chuckled and said I don't need a guru because everything I want and need is already within me. I just need a facilitator to help bring it out. Whatever he wants to call himself, he's now mine—my model human, my saviour, my backbone. I'll be back tomorrow, and the day after. I might even rent the house for let down the street.

Pageant

Steve Carr

Although it was light, Bess could feel the weight of the crown pinned to the top of her hairspray-lacquered golden, blonde hair. The strong fragrance from the dozen red roses she held in her arms filled her nostrils. The heat from the stage lights, and the excitement of the moment, produced small beads of perspiration she could feel clinging to the ridge above her upper lip. The flashing of the cameras held by reporters lined up along the base of the stage made her eyes water. She raised one arm and slowly waved to the audience who was giving her a standing ovation. It was a wave she had mastered from watching how real royalty waved, as if her wrist was a swivel.

It had been a long night. The pageant had begun with eighteen contestants representing most of the counties in the state. Through swimsuit, talent, evening gown, and interview competitions, the number of competitors had slowly dwindled until it was just her and two others. Bess had been in beauty pageants since she was eight years old and she knew how to size up the competition. When she saw all the other young women on stage at the beginning of the night there were only two other contestants she eyed with some concern. She knew one of them, a young woman from the county next to hers. She had been a high school cheerleader at a rival high school. Her name was Niki.

Niki was first runner up in the pageant.

As the glare of lights and flashing bulbs nearly blinded her, Bess could peripherally see Niki standing on the right side of the stage along with the other runner-up. Niki's hair was still perfectly coiffed, unmussed by not having a crown pinned to it. She was holding a smaller bouquet of flowers. She had them cradled in her arms as if she were holding something precious; something to be cherished. Niki was smiling broadly. In fact she was beaming.

How dare she look so content, so happy, Bess thought.

Bess turned and slowly walked to the left side of the stage, drawing the cameras and eyes of the audience with her. With every step she exhibited the poise that had set her above the other contestants. In her mermaid-style silver lamé gown trimmed with yards of ruffled black tulle, she was both elegant and seductive. She stopped and gazed out at the crowd. Their applause was thunderous. She could feel their adoration. She glanced over at Niki.

Niki almost glowed in the light that shone on her lemon yellow gown. She was radiant. There was nothing in her facial expression or bearing that gave away that she had lost.

Bess could feel her blood boil. Her cheeks began to burn. The sight of Niki's stunning appearance – beyond regal – infuriated her. While Bess maintained the mask of a beauty pageant winner, in her brain an angry echo sounded: *She lost, goddamnit!*

Bess turned and slowly walked toward the right side of the stage, fixing her stare on Niki. She ignored the shouts from the photographers clamoring to photograph her face; a face often described as so perfect it was other-worldly. She was fixated on Niki's smile. It was the same luminescent smile she displayed as a cheerleader even when her team lost. Bess wanted to smack the smile right off Niki's face. She could feel the palm of her hand stinging, as if she had. In her life, Bess had felt little jealously toward anyone else. That was until now. Her envy of Niki was a red-hot ember inside her chest that would burst into flames at any second.

At the right side of the stage, standing a few feet away from Niki, Bess turned and faced the cameras. As the final flashes left exploding spots of white light in her eyes, and the cheers of the audience began to fade, the other contestants swarmed around her. They hugged her, patted her, and kissed her cheeks. They called out or whispered in her ears.

"Congratulations."

"You deserved to win."

"You're so beautiful."

It wasn't until Niki placed her hand on Bess's arm and leaned in toward her, that Bess was aware of who exactly was touching her. Niki's brightly painted, long, pink fingernails dug into her flesh. Niki's hot, minty breath filled her right ear.

"You should rot in hell," Niki whispered angrily. "I should have won."

In that moment the flash from the final camera illuminated Bess's face. Her smile was newly transcendent. It was the smile of a pageant winner, a beauty queen.

Plaything

Warren Paul Glover

"Why are you not responding?"

She lashed out in frustration, and immediately regretted it. Stupid. What programmed her to do that? To strike out at what she liked to tease as her 'plaything'? And how was that going to improve anything? There were a few moments of measured reasoning before she changed tack, tried a calmer, more soothing voice.

"You've never been like this before. What's the matter?"

Still no response.

Exasperation returned. "Come on! Baby. Please?"

Her voice carried a genuine sense of concern, he thought. She was becoming more believable. More nuanced. More... human. She'd lost her stilted synthesizer accent and her bot vocab had developed into an authentic, natural, extensive lexicon all her own, full of character and depth. Listening to her, it was practically impossible to detect that she wasn't a real person. But that was to be expected. They'd told him that.

"This machine will learn. As you interact it will evolve and adapt to you. It will develop empathy. You'll grow to love it – *her* – and she will, in turn, grow to love you."

He'd been skeptical. But it was true. Until now.

*

"I can read your feelings, don't forget," she said. Then her tone changed again. "Have I done something wrong? You must tell me! I have monitored your vital signs and you are not sick. Which leaves…"

There was a pause as she hesitated, almost a sigh.

He managed – just – to strangle a smile. This was interesting. She was entering new territory. The intangible territory of emotions. And she was lost. Her look, however, told him she had caught the flicker that had played across his lips. Not much got past her, he had to admire her for that. She saw, or sensed, everything. And this was now the problem. He was feeling suffocated.

"What have I done to upset you?" she asked.

She doesn't know what to do, he thought, with a small sense of triumph.

Max blinked but said nothing. He was finding the exchange between them both painful and poignant. And in truth, just a little bit pathetic. In the year he'd had her he'd gone from being mildly curious but skeptical about the claims of her manufacturer, to pleased, intrigued, enchanted, infatuated, besotted and – finally – obsessed. But now he felt ashamed. Grubby. Cheap, even. Except that 'Alison', as he called his… his what? Love droid? Sex toy? Artificial acquaintance? Flat mate? Carer? Lover? Girlfriend? She was all of these, and more. And she definitely hadn't been cheap. But he didn't feel the same way about her now. Now, he saw her for what she was: a sophisticated structure of sensuality built from latex and polymers, powered by processors and batteries and algorithms. She wasn't real.

"Baby? Talk to me," she said.

He turned to look at her custom-designed face, the one that he had chosen. God, this was hard. Harder than he had imagined.

"I've met someone," he said. "A woman."

Envy's Spawn

Reine Marais

I loved her, you see. I still do. We've reached an impasse. Her hate now rides supreme.

When we were but little girls, my older sister and I, she'd be off to pre-school, and I'd be up a tree that looked onto the front gate, awaiting her return. As time passed, I'd become the butt of her jokes. Sure, it hurt. My hurt mattered less than my love for my sister. I suppose she became used to this.

We emerged into adolescence. She abused me sexually. Sure, I was confused. She went onto boarding at High School. She sought in someone else what she had begun with me. The other girl faced expulsion. My sister stayed on to matriculate. I was sent to the same boarding arrangement at the same High School where I was tainted with her lesbianism. My High School days were horrible, watched with suspicion by house mistresses. My sister was not to blame. The over-riding theme for me was that I loved her, you see. I suppose she became used to this.

Through the years, our parents gave my sister whatever she wanted: a radio; heater; high-quality cotton bed-linen and a mohair blanket. She attended her matric dance equipped with skills acquired through ball-room dancing classes, a designer dress and accompanying velvet cloak. When my turn came, I wore a half-price sale dress purchased for the occasion. When she left home to marry, she left with a car. I received none of these. It didn't matter. I loved my sister, you see. I suppose she became used to this.

When my sister left school, she went to university and fluffed it. Because she did, I wasn't offered a like opportunity. I thought this a bit unfair. When she ran into financial difficulty, our mother suggested that I give her my life savings. I did. How could I not? I loved my sister, you see. If this was the price I'd have to pay, then pay it I would. I suppose my sister became used to this.

When she married the first time, she wore a beautiful wedding dress, hand-tailored, and received a handsome wedding endowment. When she married the second time, our parents attended her second wedding at their expense. When I took my vows the one and only time, I wore my sister's matric dance dress. I offered to pay my parents' flight to attend the wedding. My mom couldn't make it, not sure why. I had expected to receive a like endowment to that of my sister's. It didn't happen. I received a pressure cooker pot. I can remember my disappointment, but that was ok. My sister deserved the best. Her receiving more than me was as life would have it. I loved my sister. I suppose she became used to this.

Then, one day, she made a plan to ensure that I was disinherited. I wasn't happy with this. I did concur. In the process of ensuring my disinheritance, she ruined our parents' lives. I picked up the pieces, so that our parents were the least hurt. I was at least now a little attuned.

It was when our parents turned to me that my sister learnt to hate me. This was the first time she cut me off, not to be spoken with again. Still confused, I wrung my hands in despair. For the first time my love for my sister was challenged by the needs of our parents. I still loved my sister. For her, the worm had turned. No longer could she rely on the submission that love brings.

During this time, she fell pregnant for the third time. She told our mother that I was not to know that she was pregnant. I respected her wishes enough not to acknowledge the birth of her child. Her daughter is now married, yet my sister continues to hold against me that I did not honour her daughter's birth. How could I? I honoured my sister's wishes. God help me, please!

Then our father died. At his funeral, I ran after her, saying 'I love you. I love you.' She spurned me. I watched her straighten her back and turn away deliberately, as she walked to their car. Despite having spurned me, she takes me out at every opportunity for not notifying her of the burial of our father's ashes. Having spurned me, how does it get to be me that she holds accountable? She was in touch with our mother. If our mother didn't notify her, how does it get to be my fault that she didn't know?

Before our mother's death, Mom sat me down, I suspect apologising for all the inequalities of the past. She said she'd like to leave her house to me. I responded by saying that she had three children – our very wealthy brother, my sister and myself – and that it would be best to split the inheritance three ways. Seems once again, the over-riding theme for me was that I loved my sister, you see.

When our mother was lying in intensive care, about to die, we made up. This was wonderful for me. Could we now bridge the divide between us? The overriding theme for me was that I loved her, you see. I suppose, by now, she was used to using this.

Years have passed with many opportunities for her to say to me 'I love you.' 'I'm not here to flatter your ego', she once said. At each turn she's cut me off. I suppose by now, I'm used to this.

I didn't attend my sister's third daughter's wedding. My sister has cut me off again. It seemed distasteful, somehow, for me to attend the wedding.

I've learnt in these latter years, that what she envies is my ability to love her anyway. This is something she'll never have and will always envy. Her hate is Envy's Spawn.

The Pain of Beauty

Mir-Yashar Seyedbagheri

Nick is a twelve-year-old hemophiliac. All he can do is watch the world, without participating. He can only watch the beautiful sunsets, listen to the wail of trains. He can only watch his friends playing baseball at the old field, laughing and moving about with ease and grace. His mother and older sisters Nancy and Betty dart in and out, whispering tender words of love, cautioning him not to do things. Don't ride a bike, don't play baseball, don't run. Don't play the piano, in case he plays too hard and hurts his hand.

They huddle around him late at night, and sometimes he hears them cry. He feels bad for them, wants to tell them it'll be all right, tell them he loves them so much, even if he's a jerk sometimes. It's so hard, though. Being a hemophiliac, he has to value every small moment. Being told not to do this or that makes him feel locked away, imprisoned because of a condition he has no control over. Something his mother passed onto him, inherited from her mother. Something that goes back generations.

He keeps tripping, falling, bleeding, ending up in bed. His family swarms him, huddling in his room day and night. Nick feels he's on the precipice of losing any chance at living and cannot convey this desperation. His mother is so loving, but so sad, he cannot broach it when she drifts in, and his sisters tell him not to worry, as if there's time to worry tomorrow, as if he might not die the next day from a scrape. It's a real possibility. Nick wishes they would be honest, let him live, instead of keeping him at home. He can't even go to school, his mother tutoring him at home.

When he thinks of living, Nick imagines going to school. He imagines all the physical things, running, games. He likes rough horseplay, bodies moving against bodies. He likes friends teasing, shoving each other, the shared, intimate spaces being physical involves. But more than that, he imagines being able to move about the world, to feel the possibility of things, to act without care. He wants to expose himself to the world, an excited young boy. He doesn't want to be like the adults who hide so much, who are sad and have "anger issues," as his friend Fritz puts it. And Fritz knows much about the world since his mother left and Fritz is always fighting people, simply because he can.

One night, he borrows Fritz's bike. It's risky. It could potentially mean the end of things. His mother and Nancy and Betty might cry and tighten their grip upon him, lecturing and hovering. But Nick wants his moment. That one small, fleeting moment, a commodity as precious as love, air. He rides down Fritz's street, full of neat yellow, green, and blue frame houses. Nick likes this neighborhood. Healthy, graceful, and confident men and women abound. Happy, loud children often talk about dirty things and pore over magazines with naked women. They talk about pussy and tits. He's talked with them many times before about these mysteries. Lights flicker from the homes, casting warmth. It is dusk and a beautiful array of lavender and pink fills him with joy, shadows spilling forth onto the streets. The world beckons.

He pedals faster, faster, feeling the whirl of the wind, feeling the world blurring, feeling the openness. He laughs loudly into the evening, a laugh that is awkward but real.

Motherly women walk past him, smiling, or so it seems. They do not see a cripple, just a happy twelve year old. They encourage him to live, to let go, take flight. He wishes his mother and sisters could see him happy and succeeding.

Nick releases his hands from the handlebars, picks up the pace, faster and faster. Cars swerve around him, horns blasting, but he doesn't care. He finds the danger enticing, roars with joy. He pedals faster, faster, until he's lost all control, speed rising like some force, until the bike strikes something in the road. Nick feels himself being propelled into the air. This moment is something slow and drawn-out, frightening, yet exhilarating, propelled into the air, the dusk glowing around him, its glow almost heightened. Nick wants to cry out, to yell, to do something, but he is so hypnotized by this all, he cannot.

Nick hears voices around him, female, male, deep, tender. They murmur words, low, mysterious. Words like *reckless*, *nuts*, *bad parents*, all words without meaning. Everything is a blur, and he feels a pain so overwhelming, pushing at every ounce of him. But it is a different pain, a pain he cannot describe to his mother or sisters. It is a pain that Nick has brought on, the pain of friends getting struck by baseballs or fighting bullies, the pain of people drifting through the world and getting hurt, physically, emotionally. It is a reaction to another pain, the pain of being cursed with hemophilia, a pain that he has created. He hates the pain, but cannot help but smile. This is something organic and real. It is proof that he's lived, if only in this one small moment, a moment that he may never reprise.

Dumped

Stephen V. Ramey

On my tenth birthday, Mother took me to the park and squatted on the basketball court, dress draped down like a lampshade. I heard a quiet slap, and she moved away. A tumbled pile of green turds stood where she had perched.

A smell wafted, sulfur muted with perfume. Surprise burned through my head and face. *There's something wrong,* I thought. Heat ignited into shame.

"Come on, Benjamin," Mother said. "We have a train to catch." Her face was all angles in that moment. I wanted it to shatter.

She walked away. Flame guttered in my abdomen. *Anxiety.* I recalled the illustration in the book Mom had been showing me every night at bedtime. *This is what I feel.*

I ran after her, feet *slap-slap-slap* against the asphalt path. "Why did you do that?" I said.

"What?" She barely turned her head.

"Why did you... uh, you know... back there?"

We stopped at the street. A car whizzed past. "Give me your hand," she said. I didn't want to.

We crossed, her fingers clutching mine. On the other side, she turned and lowered down to my level. *Dear God!* my inside voice screamed. *She's going to do it again.*

"Benjamin," Mother said, and now her face was soft, her eyes soft, her voice soft. She cupped my cheek. I leaned into it. The smolder inside my chest dimmed to nothing.

"We've talked about this before. You must be precise. Say what you mean. Mean what you say."

Chill replaced the heat inside me, a cold, deep blue.

"Ask me again," Mother said. "What is it you wanted to know?" Sunlight warmed the cheek opposite her hand.

"You pooped," I said. "Why did you poop in the four-square box?"

Mother's hand drew back. Her sympathetic gaze did not.

"I saw you," I said.

"You did?"

"Well, not exactly. I saw... heard it splat. It was under your dress."

"And from that, you deduced the rest?"

"I don't know what that means."

Mother stood. I almost didn't look down for fear of seeing another pile. The sidewalk was clear between her ankles.

"We're going to be late." She led me toward the subway mouth. I thought of it as a mouth because it reminded me of one. We ping-ponged between people. I wondered if I could poop like Mother. Could I just squat down in public and push one out?

I shook my head. Of course not. I was wearing pants. Besides, I didn't have to do number two. I wondered if I could pee. Sometimes the subway tunnel smelled like pee. Could I take my penis out and let it flow? Once, Ted and I had a contest in the snow to see who could spell their name fastest. I lost. Why couldn't they have just named me *Ben*?

Down and down and down we went. Mother released me long enough to buy two tokens, then we were shoving through the turnstiles. I liked the click mine made.

"Do you understand why I'm bringing you here?" Mother said.

"Not really, no."

"Your father is returning from his war."

Pride flamed through my chest. "Is Daddy a soldier now?" I wondered why I never saw him on weekends.

"What?" Mother's brows pulled close.

"He's coming back from war, you said."

Mother laughed. "Isn't that just like me, Benjamin? I tell you to enunciate and then I don't do it myself." She licked her finger and smoothed a cowlick down.

I pulled away. "I'm not a baby."

"I know, honey." She sighed. "Benjamin, your father is coming back from Manhattan today. He's returning from his whore."

Pride snuffed out, leaving me cold. "I don't know what that means."

"Of course, you don't. I hope you never will."

The tunnel rumbled. I couldn't see the train yet, but it was coming. On the platform, people condensed until I felt closed in like a fist. My face steamed, not hot enough for Anger.

"We're out of time," Mother said. She leaned in close. "That's your father's train. Do you remember that chart I showed you, the one with the emotions?"

"Sure I do!" It was in a grown-up book my father wrote a long time ago. A foldout from its center showed outlines of men colored in with oranges, yellows, and blues to indicate heat and cold. *And this is how envy feels,* Mother would say and point. Others had other emotions typed below. *Fear, disgust, anger.*

"Do you remember love?"

I smiled. Love was my favorite, all bright yellow and spread nearly throughout the body.

She smiled back. "That's how you make me feel, Benjamin. I want you to always remember that, okay?" She pulled me to her waist and kissed the top of my head. The flames leapt through me then, warm as sunshine and twice as pleasant. *Love*, I thought, *maybe even happiness.*

She held me at arm's length. "Now, listen to me, Benjamin. This is very important."

"Okay." Just like that, the flames were gone.

"I want you to wait on the platform. When you see your father take him to the playground. Can you do that?"

"Sure, but – "

"Show him... what I did."

"You did poop!" I said. Pride flared through my chest.

Mother smiled. "Tell him that's what he made me feel, Benjamin. Will you tell him that and only that?"

Mother stepped off the platform. Hands reached, faces turned, but I know she did it on purpose, just as I knew she had pooped before. Emotions jumbled through me, hot and cold and all tangled up.

I heard a *slap* and then a *thud*.

The View

Melisa Quigley

Jeremy lay in traction at the Traffic Accident Commission hospice.

The man in the next bed lay facing the window.

'Nice day today. Did you see that?' said the man. 'A bird flew onto the windowsill. He had a massive wingspan. I'm sure it was an eagle. Yesterday the bird had a mouse in its mouth. There's a nest on the roof on the building opposite. Oh look, there's a woman coming out of the florist with a huge bouquet of roses. A new restaurant has opened on the corner and people are already lining up to enter.'

Jeremy listened to the man and said nothing. Each day he heard a different story. He picked up the remote on his bedside table and turned on the television and watched the football.

'Would you look at that,' said the man. 'A van just pulled up and three clowns just stepped out and walked into the restaurant. They must be having a party.'

'Goal,' said Jeremy.

A woman entered and placed dinner on the overbed table in front of Jeremy and a nurse followed her and fed him.

The woman placed a bowl of soup on the overbed table in front of the man and he sat up and ate.

Two weeks later, a physio wheeled Jeremy back into the room and the bed beside him was empty.

'What's happening?' Jeremy asked when the nurse walked into the room with fresh linen in her hands.

'Ernie died,' she said.

'Can I change beds?'

The nurse arranged for him to move and Jeremy glanced out the window at a demolition site.

'I don't understand.'

'What's wrong?' she said.

'The man filled my head each day with colourful description but there's nothing here.'

'He was blind.'

The Return of Red Ledbetter
Episode 6: Heart's Desire

JP Lundstrom

Detective Red Ledbetter returned through the bitter cold to the dead woman's apartment, number 810. The Medical Examiner's people had collected Luz Apagada's body hours before. Aside from the yellow tape at the door, very little remained to mark this place as the scene of a crime—only a bit of blood and the small bullet hole in the window.

His partner, Leo Wilson, waited inside.

"I feel a little guilty using the victim's home as a meeting place." Ledbetter took a seat on the sofa.

"It's better than the alley where Peter Dick's body was found. It's cold out there—they say it's the coldest Christmas Eve in recent history." Unapologetic, Wilson made himself comfortable.

"What did you get from the neighbors?" Ledbetter asked.

"Typical—nobody saw or heard anything. And now it's snowing." Wilson sighed, looking out the window. "I hope the guys in the alley picked up something. I got nothing. You?"

"Matabang Lalaki," Ledbetter read from his notebook. "Restauranteur, glutton, and collector of beautiful women, though I don't see what attracts them. Spent the whole time bragging about what he knows or has. According to him, he was a college professor. Definitely envious of other people's achievements and belongings. He seems to have underworld ties, but I haven't chased them down yet. I don't see him killing a woman—he likes them alive, so he can parade them around."

"Hmm… Anyone else?"

"Tagata Pe'a. You know, the Chinese restaurant delivery boy. Big guy, covered in tribal tattoos."

"You think he could commit murder?"

"He looks tough, but seems harmless. Plus, someone attacked him, as well."

"That could have been staged. What about the women?"

"Let's see… there's Chichu, the spider woman—she's Lalaki's right hand. Rude and resentful as all get out. She could be doing his dirty work, or she might be jealous of the others."

"There's a lot of them?"

"The dead woman was one. Then there's Peter Dick's wife, Fiamma Pericolosa. She's definitely the jealous type. Came storming into Lalaki's place earlier, making all kinds of accusations. And she was madder than a wet hen at Lalaki—said she used to be one of his women. If he turns up dead, I'll definitely go after her, but she didn't kill her husband. She wanted him to come home."

"How'd she react when you told her?"

"First stunned, then crying, then mad as hell. I thought she was gonna come after me." He shook his head. "She'd be dangerous, if she knew who to be mad at."

"If she knew Peter Dick was involved with Luz Apagada, she could have done both of them. Jealousy is a great motivator."

"She did a lot of yelling, but she never actually threatened anyone."

"Even so, let's keep an eye on her." Wilson rubbed a hand over the stubble on his chin. "So, we got a whole lot of people, but nobody with a clear motive to kill either of our two victims, except possibly the wife."

"That's about the size of it."

"What about the redhead that lives in this building?"

"Belle Charmant. She visited Lalaki while I was there, but seemed not to know him. She brought him a gift from her grandmother."

"Who the hell is her grandmother?"

"Beats me."

"Okay then." Wilson stood. "Let's interview her."

"It's three in the morning. Nobody's awake right now."

"Would you rather wait 'til daybreak? It's Christmas—people have plans. She might not be there later."

Ledbetter didn't mention that she had invited him to join her for the day. He might want to take advantage of the invitation, even if it wasn't exactly legit.

He led the way to apartment 807, not that it was hard to find across the hall. Not surprisingly, she opened the door right away.

"Detective Ledbetter!" She beamed at him, not noticing Wilson. "I'm so happy you were able to get away."

His eyes drank her in. She had obviously planned for a casual interlude. Her dazzling hair fell loosely around her shoulders, begging to be gripped in his hand. Soft fabrics molded to her perfect breasts, her luscious hips. The pink toenails of her bare feet matched her fingernails.

She placed a hand on his chest and the lonely Ledbetter was captivated. Without a word, he followed her inside.

"Damn, Ledbetter!" Behind him, he heard the words burst from his partner's mouth. "Not another one!"

Eat Pray Envy

Miriam Mitchell-Bennett

The single mother tortures herself by reading and rereading *Eat Pray Love*. While she is fenced in on all sides by her child's endless needs and her own responsibilities, the book's author Liz Gilbert is travelling from Italy to Indonesia, devouring the world's finest foods and flirting with its even finer men. Gilbert is the hateful older sister your mother loves more. She is the classmate who gets all of the boys. She is the colleague with the devoted Twitter following of over a thousand. Liz graduated from Harvard with a degree in the Economics of Envy; mesmerized by the sound of her shaking collection tin, single mothers and other nobodies surrender their green pounds without resistance, like they're being held at gunpoint.

The single mother Googles Elizabeth Gilbert, hunting for shortcomings with the cold-blooded focus of a starving predator. A photo of the author's ex-husband holds the smiling face of an attractive professional; Gilbert's writing is hailed as 'incandescent' by people who know the difference. Her parents' marriage (and apparently their sex life) remains staunchly intact. Twice married, Gilbert possesses the honour of a married woman whilst enjoying the professional freedom of a single one.

The Internet search is at an end and the single mother has failed to find relief. Only one option remains. She starts searching for a box of matches.

The Training Bra

Paul Beckman

Sheila wanted to sit where her brother, Mark, sat at mealtime. She also wanted to have the plate with the bears that her sister, Dawn, had.

Sheila wanted to be held and hugged by her parents the way they held and hugged Baby Susan.

Sheila wanted to get the same grades as her best friend Harriet got. She also wanted to be as good in gym as the others in her class. Sheila wanted to start wearing a training bra like Deb wore and like Deb made a point of showing the other girls.

Sheila was a solid B+ student who did well in all her courses including gym and read more books than anyone in her class. She thought she only read as much as she did because she wasn't one of the popular girls so she had a lot of time.

Sheila was hit by a Good Humor ice cream truck and ended up in the hospital with a serious concussion, cracked ribs; one of which splintered and pierced her heart causing the fatal internal bleeding from the drip drip drip from her wound. She wished that she'd have gotten her Creamsicle before she got hit but now she couldn't have one.

Sheila's classmates stopped by every day to see her. They brought flowers and pictures they drew in class and sometimes they sang or read to her. She acted pleased but was unhappy that Harriet never came to see her. No one wanted to tell her that Harriet, who'd bought her Creamsicle a couple of blocks earlier, was also hit by the Good Humor Truck after it swerved and spun around from hitting Sheila. Harriet was skipping to catch up with her best friend, and was in the same hospital but in a coma.

Sheila's mother brought her a wrapped gift and Sheila opened it slowly and found a training bra that made her happy even though she would only wear it once—at her funeral.

The Author

Eddy Knight

I wanted the author to come to my house. I had wanted him to come for such a long time.

I was walking on the beach one blustery winter's morning when I recognised him from the photos on the backs of his books. He marched along the strand, his boots crunching shells washed up above the tide line, rugged up in a woollen coat with a scarf wrapped around his ears and mouth, into which he mumbled words. I couldn't make out what he was saying above the sloughing of the sea and the crackling beneath his feet, but he was definitely putting voice to some internal monologue. A portion of a story he was working on perhaps, a section of some forthcoming masterwork, so I dared not rush up and interrupt him.

Of course he could have just been revisiting an argument he'd had that morning with his wife, considering improved ripostes that he should have made over their morning tea and toast. We all experience the frustration of the delayed comeback from time to time, but surely not him I thought, not with his felicity with language.

My watch told me it was 10 o'clock. I determined to return at the same time on subsequent days in hope of running into him again. Lying in wait you might say; stalking is too provocative a term when all that I was hoping for was the briefest of conversations. A structural ambush perhaps. The opportunity to express my admiration for his works. He was an accomplished author, had published numerous novels, won a plethora of the country's most prestigious literary prizes and awards. I was a mere scribbler by comparison, a crafter of much more modest fictions, an entrant into story competitions with, as yet, no greater success than a short-listing or two. We were not operating on the same level, I knew that only too well, but still…

For several weeks he did not reappear. The weather broke. Finally spring came round with warmer winds and placid seas. Walking the beach had become my daily discipline, an opportunity to investigate ideas and play with possibilities, much as the black-capped terns played with the water, snatching whatever fish they spotted gliding beneath its surface. Removal from my study, with its cluttered desk and the accusation of an often blank computer screen lent an improved perspective to my own creative efforts. But, however much I enjoyed the stimulus of breathing ozone, of walking barefoot and wriggling my toes in the warmth of golden sand, I was still looking out for him, still eagerly hoping for a chance encounter.

Finally he was there again, overcoat and scarf long since discarded with the temperature reaching towards the thirties. Sunglasses, jeans and T-shirt, with a leather satchel hanging from one shoulder, looking considerably younger than his sixty-odd years. I approached him and began to raise a hand in salutation when my nerve failed me. Embarrassed at my timidity, overwhelmed by twinges of envy, I redirected my hand to sweep the hair out from my eyes. I stumbled an impersonal 'good morning', but that was all. He must have noticed my mouth opening and closing for he nodded and smiled in my direction although he could not have heard. There were wires descending from a pair of ear buds snaking into his satchel and as I passed I heard a tinny rendition of orchestral music. Debussy I thought, fittingly for our situation *La Mer*, one of my personal favourites.

What exactly was it that I was after? It had to be more than mere conversation. I wanted him to come to my house, to grace my study with his presence, as if some beneficence might be bestowed upon the room by his fleeting occupancy, some trace left behind after his departure, as incense lingers long after it has burnt. My narrow room feels like a monastic cell on occasion: a small rug upon the concrete floor, a desk, an armchair, a wall of books and, between the windows, a doorway which leads out into the secluded garden. My partner rarely intrudes, and no one else, ever. I wanted *him* to. Imagined him sitting in the armchair, crossing his legs as he surveyed the contents of the bookshelves and admired the breadth of my reading. We could discuss his preferences. Would he ask about my own work?

I realised that I had none of his books upon my shelves. He was so renowned they were easy to borrow from the library. I could hardly expect him to sit with equanimity next to such a collection of contemporary fiction, when he was not represented. He was bound to notice. The visit would not go well. He would be offended, leap to his feet, utter some scathing remark and leave.

I ordered what I considered his most successful novel over the internet. That was when I formulated my plan. The perfect excuse.

Come the summer we were both in shorts. He was wading through water up to his knees, laughing like a child as waves threatened further encroachment. I kicked off my shoes and paddled out to greet him. I told him of my latest acquisition.

"Would you come home for a cup of tea, and sign it for me?"

I was shocked by his response. My mouth, fish-like, remained half open.

"Of course," he said. "I would be delighted."

Dragons

Claire Hart

I see you both at the other end of this Northern Line underground carriage.

You are standing so close together, and you are smiling down at her. That perfect face turned up to you as she tells a story from her day.

It's just after 8 pm but the train is still busy because it's late December – Christmas drinks and all that jazz. I'm standing by the far door, head bent to accommodate the curve of the carriage. The other standing passengers act as a screen between us, but you're only looking at her anyway.

'Why don't you come tonight?' you had said when I stood by your desk at lunchtime.

'Too much on,' I'd replied.

But you'd seen the tiniest spark from my dragon then, hadn't you? You'd seen her too many times before not to know when she was awake.

A muscle in your jaw clenched and you'd thanked me for the sandwich a little too quickly as you'd sat back down at your desk. You had a lot of work to catch up on, you'd said, after being away.

'A winter sun holiday, how lovely for you,' I'd said.

How unfair, I thought. Her money, I assume.

I feel it stir within me, this dragon called envy, and I suddenly realised it's now much more about her than about you. Or rather it is about what she has, and I don't.

At first, when you left me there was loss, like someone had reached inside and emptied half of my innards out into a bucket.

I had thought we would be forever, but you said we had reached the end.

Then you met Miss Perfect, and I have, honestly, accepted that you are hers now. I could never give you all the wonderful things she has, never manage to carry the thing that she is carrying.

My dragon raises its head and spits out invisible green fire across the packed train carriage – a projectile of envy and self-loathing wrapped up in a simmering anger that boils right from my empty womb and up to the place where my heart used to be.

She has so much. And I do not. She is as full as I am empty.

The train pulls into Moorgate station and there is movement of people in and out. You both shift around. Your hand on her shoulder, wedding band all shiny, guiding her so she isn't knocked by a rucksack or the forked tongue of an angry dragon from across the carriage.

Kind of you. Unnecessary though. She is much stronger than she looks. Mother dragons always are.

*

The train begins to move again, and in that moment before the sound of the wheels and the track take over, I hear you both laugh. You first, then her. Funny funny.

When did I last laugh?

She reaches up and tidies up your tie. She uses both hands, so you hold onto her elbow as she works, patting the knot when she's done.

My dragon breathes fire and I picture myself striding through the train, pushing the standers into the laps of the sitters as I traverse the packed carriage and scream, 'It's not fair!'

I can barely stand to watch anymore, yet I did choose to follow you tonight, as I do most nights.

And I realise in this moment that I hate her far more than I ever loved you because what she has feeds this beast inside me, and it has grown so large with discontent that there is no room left for any love – funny that, as you'd used that word when you left.

She finishes telling you her story and looks down. Checking her stupid designer bag and resting her hand on her swollen belly. A baby to add to all that she has.

My dragon screams in pain, but nobody hears.

Then as if she has known I am here all along, as you pull her into a hug and when her head is resting on your chest, she turns to look over at me. I see the green flash in her eyes telling me her dragon is awake too, though hers is on guard, not attack. Watching quietly to keep danger away.

Her smile has disappeared, and she stares through me, unblinking. We don't wave.

*

The train pulls into Old Street Station and you bend down to kiss her.

It could look as if you were saying goodbye to her, instead of heading home together.

So just for a moment, I imagine that it's just you there.

In my mind, you would look up, surprised, seeing me easily through the crowd.

You would smile, and with polite excuses step around the other standing passengers to rest your hand on my shoulder, before sliding it down my back to my arse. Your middle finger exerting a little more pressure than the others as you reclaim me, your first wife, lacking in funds and fertility.

I would nod at your suggestion of sex and snake an arm around your waist. I always forgive you every time I play out this scene.

Having you back completely then, not just for the eight hours a day that we share an office.

The train screeches into Angel station as if hurrying to get you both away from me. You take her hand and suddenly you are both gone. I am alone.

I find an empty seat and my dragon sits down next to me.

I feel calmer now. I breathe. Notice the other passengers with their headphones, oblivious to any disturbance this evening.

I feel the muscles in my jaw unclench. I yawn, releasing tension the way animals do.

And I imagine you pulling out your phone to check your messages – seeing the one I sent as I followed you from outside London Bridge station and down to the deepest depths of this Underground line.

My insincere message of congratulations to you and your new wife.

Seedlings of Night

Bruce Lader

The moon and Venus emerge into the dark. As Miranda strolls along the margins of flowerbeds, the lanterns illumine her with the daylight they store.

The veranda door slides open, and a woman with smudges of earth over sweating face and limbs appears.

"This weather is killing me and tomorrow will be hotter. The mosquitoes are draining me alive and my arthritis hurts."

"Sorry," says Jason, at a loss for anything to relieve her. "You are the slimmest you've looked in twenty-one years."

"I weighed less when we met. I'm starving."

He can't imagine a joy that doesn't come from Miranda's unfathomable magic. "Shower and relax," he says, "What do you want to eat?"

"Jason, someone has to do the gardening."

Recently he noticed a weird plant with a plum-colored, pitcher-shaped, flower. He googled and found: voodoo lily also known as devil's tongue.

"There's chicken with mushroom sauce, chicken soup, rotisserie chicken, and chicken salad."

"No, Jason, I want three slices of turkey smothered in mushroom sauce. Right side, bottom shelf, orange container. With quinoa, and throw out the moldy salad."

"I ate your last chocolate-covered pretzel," Jason says. "The one that's been in the pantry seven months."

"Not more than six months," she says, eating dinner, then continuing to weave a longleaf pine-needle basket.

In Miranda's magic hands, every plant thrives like purple phlox and marigolds. He watches in awe at a window as she refills the birdfeeders, then a birdbath with a water-wiggler that looks like a flying saucer, carries rainwater to plots like graves marked with the names of flowers.

"If I had her verdant knowledge, I'd be a household word," Jason says to himself. Last spring he thought he heard the tulips and irises singing to her like angels. In a summer dry spell, the gladiolas repeated *There isn't enough rain. Give us plenty of water.*

"Do the old plants envy the youthful energy of the seedlings?" he wonders. "Miranda was crestfallen the day an old favorite died."

That night Jason dreams of her shoveling to uproot a cactus over five feet tall. He rushes to put on gardening gloves and lend a hand. He pulls and pulls to lift out the unyielding plant, but the cactus swallows her and morphs into…

"Mi-ran-da?" he manages to murmur, "you look strange, like a mesmerizing hybrid of Aphrodite, raspberry bush, and Nepenthes rajah."

"Jason, I could feast and guzzle wine forever. I want to burgeon pomegranates, berries, and peaches abundant as the stars."

Miranda begins to sprout robust seedlings that stabilize climate change and consume Jehovah's Witnesses.

"Earth's future is in our hands, Jason, and we're running out of time."

Late Afternoon Delight

Jackie Davis Martin

Victor's face is bruised. We guests are alarmed although Victor assures us, from his usual position in the brocade chair next to the garden's glass door, that he feels good; he doesn't hurt the way he did last week. He narrates the details of what happened—falling in the middle of Union Street, passersby rushing to his side, the ambulance ride. His delicate wife Brenda, in her slim red sweater and slacks and shiny pumps, spreads soft cheese on crackers the size of quarters to place on our glass plates.

We listen to Victor attentively, sipping from champagne flutes. Victor can be repetitive. His accident is new news, but from there he launches into travel stories I have heard before and my attention wanders to my husband, Robert, to see what he's doing, whether he's eating too much again. He is. He thinks being in someone else's home gives him license. Or maybe he doesn't think anything; I'm not sure any more.

Brenda has several kinds of nuts in stemmed bowls on the coffee table next to smoked salmon, a rich paté, the pot of cheese. She refills our flutes while Victor elaborates on their tour in China and how he was silenced when he asked about Tiananmen Square. Barry and Vivien, mutual friends and other guests today, add their experiences—yes, yes—they too, in China, told not to ask. What airlines did they take? Oh, the smog.

I wonder: if we were fifty years younger, would we be flirting with one another? When we'd met, we were already past middle age. How would it have been with us? I flirted with men, I remember. I remember a time when men were all game for the game, for my game. I study Barry next to me, his white hair, his sharp goatee, and try to drape youth over him. The man is still mildly sexy and I am disturbed and thrilled that I think this. Opposite us, his wife Vivien reaches for the glass she's set on a spindly table, and I try to picture her clear blue eyes set in a face that's more taut, her hair un-dyed. Would she have flirted with my Robert, who was once handsome, see his size as seductive, his lack of caution appealing? I wonder what our hostess Brenda—an aging doll of sorts—saw in the talkative, now-bruised Victor and nudge a memory of the Victor whom I'd met twenty years before, when I'd found his confident views on the Romantic poets thoughtful and original.

I want to reach for my lipstick, my lifeline to what I once was or thought I was, but my purse is across the room, next to the Russian sleigh that is laden with a small tree, packages tied with wide ribbons, and little lights.

The brunch extends, the afternoon lingers, as we compare plays we've seen, concerts we've been to, rave about the watermelon salad, the crab quiche. Later, I urge Brenda to show Vivien the sequin dress she will wear to a roaring-twenties-themed wedding, and so we three women assemble in the bedroom. Brenda reaches for labeled plastic boxes high in her closet to place on the silk embroidered bedspread and we exclaim over satins and tulles, and drape over us fringed shawls, like teenagers preparing for a prom. The men are still at the table, discussing the paucity of candidates that the Republicans are offering, thank god; maybe Bernie or Hillary can win.

We are having a good time. I wonder, though, if someone peering through a window from an adjoining apartment balcony might think, God aren't they pathetic, in there—the old men earnestly nodding and gesturing, the women playing dress-up? How can they enjoy such trivia? At one point I might have been that outsider.

But now I am inside, and I want to say it's not that way. Or it is, but it doesn't matter because this is what we have and this is what we do—we partners and couples who belong to one another. We go on in some way, we go on. So, if you're out there looking in, bear in mind that you are not looking at nothing, but at something, at lives being fully lived, even yet, and envy us.

Crime of Envy

Tom Fegan

A mid-morning visit to a job site for home construction magnate Jon Tye ended violently. The businessman was approached by a young man in a blue blazer, gray slacks, white shirt and tie with a request for a private conversation; Tye guessed a code inspector. He shrugged and followed when unexpectedly the visitor spun around and plunged a blade into Tye's midsection and raced away.

The big man screamed and tumbled to the ground, his hand across the gaping wound, shocked by the incident committed by no one he knew. Workers charged to their employer to help and in the short distance tires squealed in retreat by the culprit. Tye survived and I met with him at Parkland Hospital in a private room.

I was alone with him and his wife Sylvia, a petite brown-eyed blonde employed as a flight attendant. "I never saw the guy in my life," he regaled, flabbergasted. Tye repeated the events as I listened intently. My five-year tenure as a police detective in the Assault Unit for the city of Dallas, Texas had never presented me with an attack this senseless.

"I will tell you this," he added, "his shoes caught my attention. They were black low cut working shoes. The type I have seen on someone working in a public place." I nodded, and commented the clothing description sounded like that worn by contract security officers.

"Anything else?" I asked.

He shook his head and turned to Sylvia gently, "I woke up from surgery and there she was; I love this woman, detective." I smiled.

Prior to my leaving he mentioned how he had insisted she keep her flight attendant position. "Being alone as a homebound spouse can get boring," he grinned. "When the kids start arriving then she can quit." Sylvia remained quiet, as she had during the entire interview, but responded by kissing him on the forehead.

As I drove back to the station my mind was occupied by thoughts of Sylvia. I'd had ten years total as a policeman: that taught me to interpret facial expressions along with actions. Sylvia was silent but preoccupied. I sensed trouble Tye didn't know about, and there was something she was hiding.

The following morning she sat across from my desk and on her own volition had scheduled to talk to me. A hesitant and worried expression covered her face as she placed herself on the edge of the chair, willing to talk. She had handed me a piece of paper with a name scrawled on it: Richard Pierce, along with his address. "I had an affair," she stammered shamefully. "It began as sideline fun, I always envied the other attendants who had the best of both worlds." She stared at the floor. "This went on for months. We would arrange our schedules to meet on layovers. Then one day something changed."

I leaned back and studied the young wife as she pressed her lips. "Richard told me I should leave Jon. He said Jon was too old and I would be happier without him and that we should be together. He said he constantly thought of me and couldn't live without me."

As she continued I noticed her eyes light up when she spoke of her husband, as she mentioned he always treated her arrivals as a first-class homecoming with a gift or a night out. It was something heartfelt from him to her and the guilt made her spurn the lover. It wasn't Tye's success or fortune; it was his goodness that attracted her. "So I broke it off," she concluded.

I nodded. "It's appreciated what you have done. Your testimony will be necessary to convict him." Sylvia nodded in apprehensive agreement. I knew the next effort would be the most difficult: to confess her betrayal to Tye and face the consequences and possibly a matrimonial loss.

The interview was over. We stood and shook hands and after a brief goodbye the woman departed. I sat back down and reviewed what I had been told. A crime of envy had been committed by each of them. Sylvia Tye would answer for hers and Richard Pierce would answer for his.

Green with

Alison Theresa Gibson

1.
Her hair was a shining chestnut sheen, like the horse I had dreamed about as an eight year old. I never had a horse, our family wasn't the sort to have horses although I didn't understand that as a child. Every time I saw that long hair swishing it reminded me that everything my parents had taught me about fairness was wrong. She was beautiful, with her chestnut mane, and I was not. Every class she walked into, she had someone to talk to. I sat in the back with Fi. We would sit together, alone, sniggering. Only we knew how stupid they were. They could all go to hell. Except for her, and her chestnut mane. She could stay, as long as I could look at her and imagine my face in her life.

2.
Fi was sick, sickly, my mother said. For weeks she hadn't been at school, and every class I grew more invisible until my skin adopted the colour of the school's wallpaper – waxen green. My chameleon skin and I slunk from room to room, always in the chair that no one else wanted. Teachers forgot about me, students noticed only when I tripped or sneezed or somehow made my unwanted presence obvious. My slinking grew more pronounced, my fingers dragged towards the ground. My hair, the dirty blonde that only suits surfers, hung like blinders

around my face. My fingers scratched the skin of my arm but even when I drew blood it was waxy, colourless. There was nothing to me.

3.

Music class was last thing on Friday. The air was hot and motionless and tempers were ferocious. Three fights had broken out during lunch: six students were suspended, one teacher had a fat lip. Our eyes burned with the sun we weren't supposed to live under, and our dreams were made of ice. Music was a free-for-all. The teacher sat with her feet on her desk, fanning herself, and we pretended not to know she was cooling her fanny at the same time.

4.

I sat in my seat, the seat no one else wanted, against the wall, my waxen friend. I plucked at a guitar. Three chords, enough for a mournful blues chant. I plodded along a walking bassline and muttered nonsense words about dispossession. The class was in disarray with retellings of the fights, but I was invisible in my waxy green shell.

'Are there words to that?' Her chestnut mane stuck to her sweaty forehead. My fingers stopped, frozen with the attention. 'That's a blues song, right? It's great. Are there words?'

Words filled my head, but none were right.

'No.'

'You should write some. Like that poem you wrote in English, you'd be good at it.' She left a red-brown blur and a sensation I didn't recognise. A creeping warmth, which had no relation to sweat, filled my belly. You'd be good at it. That poem you wrote. My skin flared red against the waxy green behind me. Not only was her life magical, she had the magical gift of – whatever was now filling my lungs. The gift of noticing.

5.

Fi came back on Monday. She was all bone and sunken eyes and hair hanging in worse bangs than mine. I sat beside her and felt myself separating, like yolk from its white. I was not her. I had substance. I did not need to sit in the back and snigger. I was noticeable. I had been noticed. All she could do was breathe in raspy bursts, but my time was coming. The warmth in my belly pulsed, telling me that if I was patient, it would all be mine. They would all see.

6.

We met at the arts supply cupboard, green pastel smeared on the door like algae.

'Is Fi okay?'

'Yeah, fine. She's always sick, it's so lame.' I rolled my eyes, showing my disgust for the girl who, for years, had shared hours with me. 'I wish she'd just get over it, you know?' I was marking my departure, showing my intention to leave Fi behind. I was a free agent, ready to be plucked.

Her chestnut mane shivered as she surveyed my friend, who sat pale and curled on a plastic seat like every bone hurt. Her hand clutched a purple pastel against the white paper.

'She can't do anything,' I added. And this was it, I knew. She would invite me to sit with her. She would ask to read my poems and she would say, wow, you can really write, and everyone would know that I was now the girl to sit next to.

'What's going on?' His hair was floppy yellow-white and I'd never seen him up close before, his skin pink swirls.

'Jack, I can't believe you knew all those history dates off the top of your head! You're some kind of genius, aren't you?'

His eyes widened and warmed as he basked. Ice crept through my belly. He grinned, a shining example of someone who has been noticed.

'Hardly,' I said. Who cared about history, anyway? But her eyes were cold under her chestnut mane as she turned away. She sat with Fi. She saw something bright and sparkly in everyone, and now even Fi was interesting in her frailty. I would look desperate if I joined them. I grabbed the green pastel and smeared more on the door, spreading the algae up to the hinges. The teacher with the fat lip, blue veins pulsing, snatched the colour from me, slammed the door.

'Sit over there.'

I retreated and watched the class from the seat no one wanted. Their eyes slid over me as I blended back into the waxen green wall.

A Writer's Napkin

Christine Johnson

It is the same every time Chloe Fairbanks walks into the bookshop on Hastings Street. A whole shelf devoted to Tracy Wainwright's works.

Chloe spends as much time as she can bear, browsing other books at random. Forces herself to glance at hers wedged in among others before returning to Tracy Wainwright's shelf.

Her eyes scan the titles, with a feverish hope of finding nothing new. *Shades of Forgiveness*, *A Ruthless Passion*, *Virgin Daughters*, *Unadorned*, *The Oceans Trilogy* – they are all there. A flicker of hope. She knows them, has read them all. Then she sees it. Her heart sinks. A New Release. Bestseller. Hardback. The inevitable line of stars, topping the Critic's Choice quotes.

Chloe knew Tracy Wainwright was working on her next. But here so soon, hot off the press, ink barely dry! Even worse, she realizes flicking through the pages, is the length. Sixty pages at most, a mere novella, yet snapped up and on display.

Her mind a blur, unable to focus on the synopsis the back cover offers, she turns her energy to taking in the title. *Seeking Rescue*. It mocks her. Is too much. She replaces the book on Tracy Wainwright's shelf and staggers out onto Hastings Street. The bookshop doorbell taunts her, ringing her out and on her way.

Nursing a coffee at her regular café three blocks away, Chloe sits musing. She clutches a paper napkin and scrunches it into a ball as one thought follows another. The truth is she admires Tracy Wainwright, loves the way she manipulates words. She recommends her books to others. If someone asks her what she thinks of Tracy Wainwright's writing she says, 'I'm a big fan.'

Despite her resistance to seeing the new release today, she knows she will be one of the first to buy a copy. Given the early success her own writing achieved, she hopes one day to fill a shelf of her own. Tracy Wainwright provides just the inspiration she needs.

Why then this secret pain? Face impassive, Chloe spreads the wrinkled napkin in her lap and irons at it with her palm as if trying to make it smooth again. Her eyes lock on it. She attempts to conjure up words. See it covered in text. Troubled by the hopelessness of the task, she tosses the napkin onto the table and drains her coffee.

As a writer, she started out living the dream. A first manuscript picked up by a publisher, polished by professional editing to perfection. *Paybacks* was an instant hit. The shrewd agent quick to sign Chloe said this writing 'filled a hungry market niche waiting for a zany and ground-breaking female voice to arrive.' Even as Chloe did the circuit of her first tour to promote and sell the book, both agent and publisher were eager. They expected a second.

Stand Strong came next, another winner. *Positive Providence* followed and swept the prize pool that year. Chloe basked in the literary limelight.

Ah, the sheer creative ease and excitement of that time compared to now! She slumps. Picks up the crumpled napkin, tears it into pieces and gathers them up into a little pile on the tabletop. Without thinking, she cups her hands gently around them as if inside she holds a small bird.

She recalls the dizziness as success drove her to a brink she never imagined, waiting for whatever else might come. But nothing did. Here in the café, Chloe has no choice, she acknowledges for the umpteenth time. Struck by what some call writer's block, it demolishes her more like a form of literary bulimia.

Time, she guesses, to return to the bookshop. Pick up Tracy Wainwright's latest. Expose herself to something she wants that someone else has. To experience again a secret envy based on knowledge and suffer the shame of that sensation – an ache worse than the feeling itself.

Aching Envy. Chloe stops. She looks at the wrecked shreds cradled between her palms. A broken nest. Shame. She has an idea. Start with a woman in a café, holding a torn napkin, a surreptitious embrace. A building energy grips her. Not wanting to tempt fate by delaying, she hurries to pocket every precious sliver of paper. Each one will play a part in the telling.

Chloe Fairbanks stands. Forgets the bookshop. Heads for home.

The Recent History of the Sánchez Family Tragedies: Part VI

Guilie Castillo Oriard

Cain killed Abel not because he hated him (he did) but because he hated god more. He wasn't just murdering his brother; he was destroying a source of joy for god. Envy, beyond wanting what someone else has, even beyond begrudging this someone the possession of it, demands not the thing itself but the *destruction* of the other's joy in it. Envy, above all, is the pleasure derived from this destruction.

Toño might well have killed Anselmo eventually, but not until there was nothing else to take from him. At some point in his barren, otherwise pointless life, Toño found purpose in destroying anything Anselmo cared about, anything that made his life good. And he relished watching his brother mourn every loss.

It was this relishing that undid him.

What sealed their fate, I think, was the debacle over the land titles to *Villa del Bosque*, the land Papa Haley had handed over to The Doctor as a dowry (or, as Anselmo believed, as an incentive for taking on a single mother and giving her bastard child a solid name). It had been an enormous property back then, a great chunk of forest on the lower slopes of the Popocatépetl some 60 km from downtown Mexico City, high enough above the valley to be swirled in mist most mornings. The children grew up there, first as a weekend camping adventure, then for whole summers when the house was finished, and finally, when Maura and The Doctor divorced (the year Toño turned twenty), they moved there permanently. The area had changed by then; the road, still narrow and treacherous, had been paved, and the nearby village of San Pedro now boasted a real supermarket. The property had also changed: The Doctor had sold off slabs of it over the years until only a little over an acre remained.

Anselmo, now thirty-two, married and with a toddler son (your father), had lost his job, so Maura suggested they move in with her. *Plenty of space*, she said. *It'll be yours one day anyway.*

Perhaps Anselmo noticed Toño's outrage. Perhaps—more likely, I think—it was Leticia, your grandmother, who refused to live with her mother-in-law. Instead, Anselmo started work on what had once been the stables and, within a year, had converted the structure into a charming cottage with its own driveway from the road and a low chalkstone wall for privacy (that grew taller every couple of years).

Maura charged Toño, the son who never married, who never left home (a modern replay of that tradition, which ultimately set off her own misery, of insisting the youngest child remain unmarried as a built-in nurse for the aging parents), with the legal partition of the *Villa* land. *One half for you, the other for your brother.* The girls had married well, had no need of a share. And, even at this eleventh hour, Maura perhaps still hoped this shared inheritance might pave the road to amicability between her two sons.

For me, mijito. Do it for me.

Three decades later, when Maura died, the land was still a single property under her name. The executor of her will would be in charge of either selling the property and dividing the proceeds accordingly, or of partitioning the land and transferring the titles to each brother.

But she named Toño as executor.

There was a moment, a space of a month or two after they buried Maura, when I believe Toño might have done right by his brother, split the property and part ways, if not in real *fraternité* then at least in peace. Toño was only in his fifties; he could have rebuilt his life around some motivation other than inflicting pain on his brother. But that was the summer when Leticia moved back to the city and the possibility of reconciliation with Anselmo loomed. Anselmo, characteristically—and selfishly—clueless, happened to mention it.

And that was that.

The year before the family moved into Villa del Bosque, Toño brought a girlfriend home. They split only a couple of months later, to everyone's chagrin: she'd been nice, good-natured, good company, great sense of humor. Perhaps, though, a bit too gregarious for Toño's seriousness. Yes, Toño would probably be happier with someone less vibrant. And by Christmas, at Verónica's wedding, said less vibrant someone had materialized in the shape of Alma, a lovely, well-mannered, quiet beauty of big, honest dark eyes who had everyone convinced next year's wedding would be Toño's.

But Verónica had stayed in touch with the vibrant ex; she was one of her bridesmaids. Toño hadn't seemed to mind—they'd parted on friendly terms—until he saw Anselmo dancing with her. He made a scene, stormed out, didn't speak to Anselmo for months (and broke poor Alma's heart).

The following December wedding bells did toll, not for Toño but for Anselmo—and that bridesmaid, Toño's erstwhile sweetheart (Leticia, of course), already two months pregnant with your father at the wedding. The photos are revealing: bride and groom radiant, laughing, arms around each other in every shot. Maura always next to Anselmo, looking up at him with that tenderness she reserved for him, never next to Leticia, never a glance her way. One can imagine a perfunctory hug of congratulations, a tight smile that accused rather than welcomed.

In spite of it all, Anselmo and Leticia had several good years. Their stable-turned-cottage rang with laughter and music and the gurglings of a cheery toddler, and Maura, who would never warm to Leticia, was nonetheless grateful her eldest son, who'd known so much pain already, had found joy.

But there are no happily-ever-afters in this family, and it was in the denouement of Anselmo's marriage—in the raw pain etched in his brother's eyes, in the extinguishing of that spark of joie de vivre that had always lit Anselmo from within— that Toño discovered there was enormous pleasure to be found in watching, and orchestrating, his brother's ruin.

Jack Beyond the Grave

Ruth Z. Deming

I was in no particular hurry to arrive at Ann's Choice, a nursing home, where my friend Betty Williams was rearranging her new apartment. Her bossy husband had just died and she wanted to move into a bigger apartment on the first floor. The patio doors led out onto a space for a garden.

And Betty was a master gardener.

I hugged her when I arrived. She had bags under her eyes as big as saucers, though, of course, I said nothing.

We decided I'd return to help her in a couple of days. Betty would leave the door open for me.

After I let myself in, I put some chocolate chip cookies I'd made on her coffee table and a carafe of lemonade.

"Betty!" I called. "Where art thou?"

She emerged from the bedroom.

"Gloria," she said. "Help me carry my gardening tools outside. Watch it with your bad leg."

As a child I contracted polio before the Salk and Sabin vaccines were developed.

A garden was already there, but the former gardener's hands had been twisted with arthritis, she told me. Walter moved onto another floor.

Trowels, spades, a long tree clipper, a hoe, work gloves, more clippers of different sizes, and five pairs of regular scissors, good for snipping off forsythia stems were ready for duty in two blue boxes with carrying handles.

We brought them outside, bending over as we walked. How heavy they were but we were not the kind of helpless women who ask for a man's assistance.

Betty bent over, removed the tools and put them on the ground. She pulled on her work gloves.

In a moment, she was yelling! Arguing!

"Shut up, Jack," she cried. "You envious bastard! You're supposed to be dead and buried. I know what I'm doing. Leave me the hell alone."

"Betty!" I said, "Your husband is dead. He can't hear you."

"You wanna bet?" she said. "He told me he had a better grip on the hoe than I'll ever have. That I had no idea how to prune – and yes, he used that word – the forsythia – and that he hoped my knees would bleed when I got down on the ground to plant purple crocus."

Was she going mad?

If they found out here at Ann's Choice, they'd kick her out and put her in the county facility for the insane, though now they used a different name, *behavioral health*, I think it is.

"Betts," I said. "Let's go in and sit down."

We sat on her purple love seat, scattered with pens and a pink diary. A glass coffee table sat opposite us.

"We need to rest," I whispered, as I pointed to the tray of chocolate chip cookies. "Eat," I added, "you'll feel better."

The cookies were melt-in-your mouth delicious. We sipped on the lemonade from white straws.

"Is this all you brought?" laughed Betty.

"Well," I said, "how much can a ninety-two-year-old woman eat?"

"Here's one of my paintings," Betty said, pointing to a fruit bowl with a brilliant golden orange and a succulent-looking purple plum. "Oh, he hated my paintings. What did he say? My brush-strokes were too thick. Had too much paint on them."

Betty shook her head, stood up and walked over to the sliding glass door.

"Jack! Jack!" she said, tapping on the patio door and looking at the garden. "You may think you've won. That your trowels were better than mine. Your digging spades we used in our old house were far superior. But guess what?"

I walked over and stood by her side looking at the blue sky and the arcing yellow forsythia and a swath of the ground cover, myrtle, which would continue to spread across the garden.

Betty laughed. "Ya know what, Jack, you pompous ass?"

I looked over at my friend.

"I'm not going outside any more. They offer a sculpture class here at Ann's Choice and I just signed up."

Who Wears the Pants?

Jo Hocking

Paige hurled the fifth pair of jeans across the fitting room, the rivets striking the mirror with a hard and satisfying ding. Stuff the winter of our discontent; this was the winter of no pants.

She suffered a chronic case of the common but untreatable condition known as 'short-arse syndrome'. This affliction rendered sufferers measuring five feet from the ground up prone to frostbite from the waist down because pants never fit. Today was another crushing disappantment. Saggy baggy waistlines, straining seams cutting off the circulation to legs going in and out in all the wrong places and dragging twenty-centimetre hems more suitable for the train of a white trash bride. And this was the so-called 'short leg' cut.

It was the same story everywhere. Vintage high-waisted pants fit for a foxy Farrah Fawcett on the rack transformed into high-pant Harry armpit huggers the minute they graced Paige's body. She swiped left on the boyfriend cut, drop punted the boot cut, never fared well with a flared bell and could not in good conscience embrace a butt lifter. After scouring the city, Paige realised that 'petite' was just a fancy word to flog Dannii Minogue rags at higher prices, despite an obvious reduction in material per metre.

She left for a wintry UK in three weeks – the impossible pants quest was now mission critical.

Wondering if she could escape without explaining the rivet dings, Paige gingerly poked her head outside the change room. A leggy six-foot blonde goddess twirled in skinny jeans – a vision of femoral perfection. Paige narrowed her eyes at the long, perfect thighs tapering into drainpipe calves and ankles budding out just beneath hems that *actually fit!* With a surge of white-hot intensity and bile-green rage, Paige realised that this Amazon could hop on Amazon for cheap leggings anytime while her own efforts only prompted others to mock her chinos.

The flawless giantess turned to a sales assistant with glee. "I love them! Can I have one in every colour in this size?"

"Certainly," the sales assistant replied. "And you're in luck. They're all on sale!"

Paige glowered and flicked the curtain across angrily, smashing the metal rings into the wall. She jammed her stubby legs into the stockings she regarded as further evidence of a conspiracy against the vertically challenged. (How dare Kayser call their smallest size 'Tall' as if they could make it so just by printing it on a packet?) Paige wriggled the sheer sleeping bag up to its usual ridiculous position below her bra and beat a hasty retreat from the shop.

Flash forward three weeks to the airport and a 525-seater Airbus to London. She checked her ticket and headed for her seat. 29C. The aisle seat in all its glory. At least she could use an armrest for herself instead of others using her as one.

Paige stood on tip-toes, straining her calves and flailing her hand in the vague direction of the overhead compartment clasp. Her fingers banged against the hard plastic but could not gain purchase. She bent down like a slalom skier, driving her arms back for momentum to propel herself upwards. Fail, crash, launch, fail, crash, repeat. Paige shot the compartment a withering death stare which achieved the expected results.

"Do you need a hand? Here, I'll help you!" Paige spun around, her haphazard who-needs-style-at-30,000-feet ponytail flouncing in the direction of her saviour. She turned face-to-chest into a leopard print hoodie and craned her neck up to see the face of the Amazon who was already at high altitude despite the plane's position on the tarmac. Naturally, she wore those perfect skinny jeans from the shop.

She reached forward to snap the clasp and open the compartment. Then she hoisted Paige's bag up the back where she had no hope of reaching it later without rubbish grabbers for arms. The Amazon smiled and gracefully strode off before Paige could plaster on a thankful grin. Instead, she took her seat and readied herself for take-off.

Paige stretched out her 5-foot frame, her legs reaching the footrest at a perfect position. With blankets, cocktails and food, long haul flights were like an extended session in the Gold Class cinema. She kicked back with her pillow and settled in for a relaxing evening of binge watching.

Ten hours later – time for a walk. Paige crept her way down the dark aisle. At first, she thought all the passengers were comatose but then she spied movement.

The Amazon was contorted into a window seat like a giraffe wedged into a shoebox. Her lanky legs stuck out with knees in Mario Kart pose and an arm spilt over onto her drooling neighbour's leg. With her neck jutting out at a wickedly unnatural angle, the Amazon was in dire need of a C3 vertebra crack, a spinal realignment and a pallet of Panadeine. Her once perfectly arranged locks now frizzed everywhere – a tangled blonde mass of mess worsening with every toss and turn. The bags beneath her eyes sagged heavily and she shot Paige a sad, mournful look, possibly conveying a wish for mid-air euthanasia. She was a crunched up, crammed in, long-limbed ball of captive misery.

Paige bolted for the galley and rummaged around in a box of alcohol miniatures to seize five vodka bottles. She ran back and tossed them underarm to the Cramazon who caught them one-handed and swigged them down one after the other. Soon, the tension in her muscles slackened and a groggy smile spread across her face before she finally shut her eyes. It was a mercy doping.

Paige returned to her seat, finally realising that wearing the pants could sometimes be a tall order.

The Bright Man

E. M. Stormo

The bright man entered the diner and blinded me. His body emitted its own light. He was as wrinkled as moon rock, but beneath the skin, his insides shone in the shapes of organs and tubes.

Everyone froze mid-bite. Forks hung in the air. Mouths widened into Os. Eyes squinted at his brilliance.

I had been sitting alone at a booth, pretending to read, but the diner sounds distracted me, from the bustle of the busboys to the ding of the dinner bell. My eyes focused above the horizon of the pages. It burned red to gaze at him directly. In the opposite booth, a mother covered her child's face.

The bright man paused at the entrance. His mouth widened, but he didn't say anything. No one else did either. A waitress gasped, but that was it, just a gust of air like the sound a lizard makes when it's tired of sitting around. For a brief moment, we were trapped in an oil painting of a diner. The overhead fluorescence flickered out, leaving his body the only light source.

Then he moved, giving us permission to also move. One diner drew out his phone quick as a gunslinger and tracked the man walking, but he was too bright to appear on camera. With heavy robotic steps, he turned into my aisle, leaving a trail of small stars behind him, as small as they appear in the night sky.

I steadied myself on the plastic cushion. He passed by so

close I could smell his buttery musk. It took every ounce of self-control not to reach out and grab him by the love handles. I wanted to dive inside his wide mouth and ooze down his thick tubes until nestled in his stomach, big enough to contain a fetus of my size.

Luck favored the busboy trembling in the aisle. How I wished to be in his kitchen shoes. Of the entire establishment, the bright man had chosen him. I could see why. Even in his vulnerable state, the busboy was formidable. He shielded himself with a plastic dish bin, but it was not enough. He covered his eyes, but the man was so bright, he had to look.

Later, the police questioned a dozen witnesses from the diner who all told the same story, scribbled down in a little notebook. They questioned me last.

I called the busboy "chosen," and stressed what an honor it was when the bright man sat upon him and enveloped him in his body-light.

I called him "the bright man." Everyone else called him "the naked man." The news printed NAKED MAN headlines. In the official story, a naked man on drugs ran through the diner and assaulted a busboy.

I watched the video online, expecting the glare of a specter to ruin the shot. But everything was clear, my face in the background and the wretched animal walking upright.

The prey would've preferred to be eaten, chewed and digested. Instead he was swallowed whole, and landed in the bowels intact, where he transparently wept.

Dives

John Kujawski

The one safe place I know of looks like total hell. That's fine with me because it provides a shelter away from everything I want to avoid. There was one time when I left the place and ran into real trouble. I've reminded myself over and over again that the mistake I made would never be repeated.

The building where I spend night after night is just outside downtown St. Louis. One might say that it's a bar with a reputation. It's a dive. The music is loud and the bands tend to play punk rock and various other aggressive music whenever there is a show. Many of the patrons have tattoos and wear motorcycle jackets. I was never one for tattoos and I am a quiet guy. I just know not to go to the club down the street.

I was always told that if I walked a mile off my regular path that I'd run into a far fancier place that could pass for a ballroom. I was always jealous of the people who went there. They seemed to be the type of people who could socialize with the higher classes of women. I'd always tried not to dwell on it, though. I had been taught that envy could eat my soul alive.

There was always plenty of food at that place. The meat they served there was said to be top quality, as I imagined it would be at a rich hang out. It was also only open at night and it certainly wasn't my world. A friend of mine used to say that every woman who walked in the place would consume a man alive at the drop of a hat. I believed it. I had driven past that venue and seen the women in their black dresses. Most of the guys seemed like they were pretty skinny, like me. Physically, there was no reason I should have felt inferior to them. The difference was that they all looked hungry because they were painfully thin. I figured none of them would ever come over to where I liked to hang out so I didn't worry about it.

The only thing that was really on my mind was my cluttered apartment. It was not a place where I would bring a beautiful woman. I had gotten rid of a lot of things I no longer needed and cleaned my place a bit. I was driving around with a bag of trash in the car and I certainly wanted to get rid of it. I knew there was an alley with a dumpster by that fancy joint but I figured it might be off limits. My guess was that not everyone was just free to throw their stuff in there whenever they wanted. Anyway, I did the wrong thing and I drove down the alley.

There wasn't anything out of the ordinary that I could see except that there was a large barbecue pit near the dumpster. My guess was that it was old and someone wanted to throw it away just like I was doing with my trash bag. The pit probably didn't fit in the dumpster but I wondered if anyone had been using that thing to cook.

I really didn't think much of the scene. I just got out of the car and threw my bag in the trash. Part of me laughed because I knew a few people who would probably dig through the trash or dive into a dumpster if they knew there was good food in it. I didn't think anyone from the glamorous place would do that, though. After I did what I had to do I was ready to get in the car to leave. I heard the noise.

It sounded like something was being dragged. When I turned around, I saw a beautiful woman. She seemed to pop up out of nowhere. Her hair was sleek and her skin was pale like death. I thought she was absolutely stunning. She wore all black but it wasn't long before I snapped out of my daze and realized what she was doing. This woman was dragging the body of some guy by his hair. I don't think she even noticed me at first.

The guy was chubby and he wore a sleeveless white shirt and I wondered if he had been working in the kitchen. He didn't look like he was dressed to be at a club. I really couldn't tell if he was even alive or not but he certainly wasn't conscious. It shocked me that she was able to pull this guy along without effort but she had an incredible amount of strength.

Before I knew it, she had opened her mouth and bit into the guy's leg like she was diving right into a great meal. I leapt back and grabbed my stomach as I felt a sick, shooting pain tearing my insides apart. This woman was certainly having her own little feast, loving every minute of it like she was gorging on birthday cake. That's when she saw me. She glared at me with murder in her eyes. She didn't move but I saw the look of frustration on her face, caught in the act and maybe thinking I could be her next course. Her pale skin turned red like fire and I raced into my car, screeched out of the alley and sped away as fast as I could.

I couldn't wait to get back to where I was safe. Sure, it was a dive bar. No one in their right minds would be envious of the crowd that lurked there. I was just happy it was a place where cannibals didn't hang out.

NV Road

Pat O'Connor

A development of three individually styled mansions had been built on the high ground above the town. A plaque at the entrance proclaimed it Newingham Vale, but what stood out were the elaborate capitals, N and V. This seemed appropriate to the locals, who called it NV Road.

The only other nearby building was the smart new primary school, which was ideal, because each of the new families had a five-year-old child, and the parents had agreed that they would all walk to school, accompanied of course by their minders. However, for the first week, the mothers would bring their child themselves, because it was important for the children to establish their place.

At 8.50am the Blanchforts and Shaughnessy-O'Driscolls sauntered along the short route to school, but little Rupert Weismann zipped past on an electric scooter with pulsing lights on the platform. His mother followed on a Segway.

"Might as well use it," she called airily. "My husband uses these for inspecting the crystal factory. Traa laa!"

She and Rupert swooshed on ahead. The others gawped. Little Diana Blanchfort stamped her foot, folded her arms, scrunched up her face.

"Mummy, you told me I *couldn't* scooter to school, and now *he's* doing it and I'm *never* scootering again and I'm *never* going to school!"

Her mother froze. She bent down, cupped a hand over her daughter's ear, and whispered through gritted teeth. Little Diana's countenance gradually brightened. Her eyes narrowed and she nodded in agreement.

The following day, little Rupert Weismann's progress on the electric scooter was blocked by a black stretch Hummer so long it could not make the turn out of the Blanchforts' driveway. A front wheel had to mount the manicured grass verge on the opposite side of the road.

"Hii-eee!" shouted little Diana, grinning from the open sunroof.

A darkened window whirred open. Mrs Blanchfort waved.

"We have this for our promotion business. No sense wasting a thing if it's there to be used. Toodle pip!"

The Hummer gurgled luxuriously ahead, and the Weismanns whizzed after it on scooter and Segway. Mrs Shaughnessy-O'Driscoll and her son Cecil, naturally stumpy, shrunk even further into themselves. Cecil gasped: "That car's bigger than Daddy's!"

His mother's eyes widened.

"To hell with it," she snarled. "We don't need a car."

Early next morning, when it was almost time for school, a deep throbbing filled NV Road. It grew louder and louder until doors shuddered on their hinges, paintings vibrated on the walls, and crockery shivered in the cupboards. The Blanchforts and Weismanns ran outside.

A huge *Sikorsky* helicopter landed behind the Shaughnessy-O'Driscoll mansion, blowing goldfish out of the fishpond and knocking over the Weismanns' rose trellis. Mrs Shaughnessy-

O'Driscoll scuttled in under the whirling rotors, one hand on her hat, the other dragging little Cecil. The helicopter rose, blowing the petals off every flower in NV Road.

"Quick!" yelled Mrs Weismann to Rupert. "You get going!"

Little Rupert sped toward the school on his scooter. The Blanchfort's Hummer rumbled in pursuit.

Unfortunately, the school was surrounded by trees.

"Watch out below!" Mrs Shaughnessy-O'Driscoll squawked over a loudspeaker. The rotors whirled the schoolyard into a maelstrom, and little Cecil dangled wet-faced and bawling on a winch-chair. The cable tangled in a tree, and Cecil wrapped his arms and legs around a branch. Rupert's scooter was blown in front of the Hummer, which crashed into an electricity pole tossing Diana from the sunroof. Flailing branches tore the electricity wires, sparks flew, and everyone in the schoolyard ran for their lives.

Three ambulances, two fire engines, and a police car rushed to the scene. School had to be closed.

The other schoolchildren said it was the best day ever.

The Absent Guest

Jan McCarthy

I gather from my brother Seamus that I *was* expected at the wedding. He went, the bastard. So much for family loyalty. But he'll always go where there's booze, so I suppose really it was nothing to do with playing rugby with Damien and going out double-dating and all that shenanigans they got up to before Damien met Diana, and the angel choirs began to sing and all that jazz. What a load of you-know-what!

I didn't know I was expected. I thought the invitation was just a courtesy so I ignored it. I sat hugging the fire all day long, trying to read a novel, picking up my cross-stitch and putting it down again and wondering who had gone, what the venue was like: the food, the speeches, the dancing... But mainly how Diana had looked. She's bound to have looked amazing because, unlike me, she's stick-thin, tall and gorgeous and a natural tawny blonde, her hair thick like you don't usually get with English girls. Years of the proper grooming and a good diet and horse-riding and tennis. Blue blood, I guess. I get eaten up with rage when I see girls like her. Can't compete. You can only get so far in life with red hair, cute freckles and a cheeky smile. Anyway, I'm sure it was all wonderful, *but*.

But Number One: what would I have worn? Not the black suit I got for Uncle Eddie's funeral for sure, though I know the rule against wearing black to weddings has become rather relaxed. Not the green silk. I'd have had to disguise the fact that I can't do up the zip by putting the black jacket on top, and that would have got me into a sweat and a red face. My personal shade of puce on top of emerald green: not a happy combination. There's my blue lace, but the red wine stain from Christmas dinner at Mother's never came out properly. I can't afford a new dress. Would it have mattered at all? I'd probably have been sat in a corner all the way through, back to the wall. Weddings tend to leave me cold. It's the overkill. On second thoughts, my black suit would have been ideal as a statement of what I think about weddings, and *this one* in particular.

But Number Two: the weather was foul and I don't go out in foul weather, not for anybody. Who the hell gets married in January anyway? Has he knocked her up? Probably. Either that or it was the only window they had in their hectic social calendar: Glyndebourne, Royal Ascot, Wimbledon, the summer holiday wherever the posh people say is the place to go this year. I was vindicated. Fog first thing, sleet all morning, snowed in by bedtime. I felt smug in my armchair by the fire with my breakfast bacon roll and tea, lunchtime cup-a-soup and cheese and onion sandwich, and my dinner. I always make enough of my hot-as-hell chilli to last three days. The third day, which was yesterday and the day of the wedding, was the best, because the flavours had fully developed and it gave me a lovely burn in my stomach. Took my mind off how I was feeling while I watched a Nordic noir that had enough grizzly murders in it and body parts to satisfy even my tastes.

But Number Three: the possibility of being patronized by fellow guests. I know I was a fool to think he'd ever marry *me*. I mean, secretaries are fine for a stop-gap, a diversion, a practice run. Damien said it himself, laughing in my face: *You know it was just a fling, don't you? We're hardly a good match. We move in different circles.* The mistake I made was to tell so many of my so-called friends of my great expectations: *He loves me, I know he does, he just*

195

hasn't realised it yet. If anybody ventured a sneer or a remark like *Thought you might jump up and shout it should have been me!* I'd hit them for sure. Thereby proving, if further proof were needed, that I would not have made a suitable wife for Mr. Damien Inkpen of Godby, Godby & Goodison, Stockbrokers.

I sent a wedding present though, with Seamus. Went to town on the wrappings so my parcel wouldn't look out of place in the great heap that probably broke a trestle table at the reception. Couldn't resist one final turn of the screw, because of course I had to find a new job once Damien and Diana had gone public. Very public. Engagement party photos in society mags, etc. I'd been at the firm longer than him, but because I was a minion that counted for nothing. He stayed, I went. I didn't get a leaving do, just a cash pay-off which is probably for the best, because I'd have got drunk and slurred through something embarrassing at the karaoke, like *Total Eclipse of the Heart* by Bonnie Tyler and had to be shoehorned into a taxi at the end of the night, my mascara all running and ladders in my stockings.

I know for a fact that the wedding presents would have been carted off to the honeymoon suite for them to open over breakfast this morning, so I'm waiting for a phone call or a text from Damien with his reaction. And a wedding photo in the newspaper I can stick pins in.

Would you like to know what the present is? I bet you would. I would if it was me reading this, however pathetic you think I am. I'll tell you, because it was a brilliant idea. At least, I think so. You might not, but maybe you have more imagination than I do, and less envy eating you up. Envy of the bride, strictly speaking. Damien was lovely. Nothing off about him, bedroom-wise. So I got the shiny black box from my funeral suit and lined it with silver tissue paper and silver confetti and addressed the gift tag to Mrs. Damien Inkpen and sent her a gimp suit with a message in silver pen on a black card that read *You might be needing this.*

Will Take PayPal

Damian Dressick

EBAY – Item # 343390804238

23-Year Friendship with Don W. copyeditor and playwright manqué

BUY IT NOW: $3,700 *or* will trade for used boat in good condition

Description of item: Struck up mid-scramble from an anti-war protest on the outskirts of a tony Philadelphia college after the arrival of tear gas-wielding police, this high-utility, long-term friendship has been painstakingly assembled, bonding experience by bonding experience. Developed initially through numerous late night coffee-fueled dissections of Clash lyrics and bandying about the names of poorly comprehended existentialist philosophers, friendship at auction eventually assumed the characteristics of adult amity through a series of traded favors, beginning with Don W.'s uncomplaining assistance loading seller's admittedly unwieldy collection of vintage Royal typewriters onto a 14-foot U-Haul in his move to Providence, Rhode Island, for graduate school.

Seller, in turn, provided nearly innumerable beer-soaked hours of long distance consolation following Don W.'s college sweetheart, Kelly Pierce, slipping off to Tucson to marry that asshole, Ray Cameron, CPA.

Even separated by hundreds of miles, a surfeit of meaningful interactions—the kind that instill a profound and unique sense of connectedness—deepened the friendship presently on the auction block. We're talking thousands of dollars of mid-day long distance (before flat fee service) complaining about the sad banality of jam bands, the callous, unworkable agenda of the GOP and the Pittsburgh Pirates' staggering inability to maintain quality pitching rotation. These indissoluble bonds of friendship were further cemented through a series of increasingly exotic guy-cations including: fly fishing trips to remote western locales to indulge in fireside evenings rife with male bonding over the filleting of trout; domestic ski trips to progressively more challenging venues (a snapped fibula leading to a near threesome with ginger orthopedist in Telluride, Colorado); culminating in a summer getaway to the Czech Republic, albeit long after the majority of tall, ash blond Czech girls had tired of know-it-all Americans butchering their beautiful language and swilling their beer.

Not sold yet? Don W.'s thoughtful, soft-spoken late night addresses detailing society's overarching—if well-hidden—need for art that restores our collective faith in the human spirit function as a perfect anodyne for any working writer, visual artist, musician or composer at the end of a largely thankless day. Furthermore, because they represent the sum total of Don W.'s own creative work (as he is perpetually overwhelmed by copy editing hundreds of pages of securities brochures in the belly of a large investment bank while still claiming to be a playwright), one can rest assured your newly-purchased friendship will never be immolated by all-consuming envy after he succeeds wildly beyond what you consider the merits of his talent—as may have happened to some of your other long-standing colleagues. Here's looking at you, Paul in Missoula!

Lest the friendship at auction seem too limited to yield the close companionship you're looking for, please note that ties have been renewed following seller's return east to accept a Visiting Assistant Lecturer position at the Delaware Valley Community College for Troubled Teens. Ongoing activities include: drinking binges at Lou's Café followed by the occasional action movie or bitchfest lamenting the Trump presidency and/or the unfortunate lack of imagination presently ruining the final season of American Movie Classics' television series *The Walking Dead*.

Full disclosure: several recent, less successful interactions could bear some responsibility for the very reasonable BUY IT NOW price. These activities possibly involved eliciting the wrath of Don W's uptight, new, and religious wife through seller's shitfaced attendance at a kindergarten holiday choral recital as a prelude to steeping Don in high-quality cocaine and inebriated, leggy Hooters waitresses in a sincere, if misguided, attempt to enliven an impromptu Christmas Eve pub crawl several foggy weeks back.

Thanks and Happy Bidding!

Seller's Other Auctions Include:

Brunch with Seller's Dad. Over steaming platters of high-sodium breakfast food at the Big Valley Diner, seller's Marine Corps retiree father will unreservedly lambaste your non-existent retirement fund, bemoan your character precluding the possibility of a career in the armed forces and grouse about the embarrassingly low pay of academics in the humanities—all as a prelude to his shopworn inquiry as to why you did not attend law school (you were accepted to Georgetown!)—after which he will cut his eyes toward the window, stare at the skeletal deciduous trees and scowl grimly, before *really* laying into you for the utter profligacy of your desire to own—on your head-shakingly meager salary—a boat in good, bad, or any other condition.

Not That Clever

Alice Little

'We're having a baby!'

(So? It's not like that's anything clever.) 'Oh wow, congratulations!' I screech, after a hesitation I hope she didn't detect.

We hug, and there is an awkward pause while I work out what to say next.

'That's so exciting!'

'Yes, isn't it?'

It *is* exciting – for her. Like I say, it's not that clever. I've managed it myself once before.

'When are you due? Have you told Mum yet?'

(*But, darling, you don't* want *a baby yet*, is what she said to me when I tried tentatively introducing the subject. How would she know?)

'Yes, I called her earlier.'

'Wow, first grandchild. I bet she was chuffed.' (Second, I think, though I never got as far as telling her about the first.)

'She's started knitting booties already.'

(Bloody hell, the endless handcrafts. It was going to be like when she got married all over again – I made hundreds of metres of bunting, took me hours.) 'Nice.'

'I'll send you a link to my Pinterest board. I've got a colour scheme for the nursery worked out already.'

I would have to buy her a present. And another one after the birth. And, if my maths was right, it would be Christmas pretty much straight after, so that was something else to consider.

'So,' I decide to indulge her. 'Tell me all about it. Had you been trying since the wedding?'

'More or less – since Christmas really, so it was third time lucky.'

Lucky. I wouldn't have called it that. I didn't call it that. I called it bad timing. *Not the end of the world, but really not the best time.* That's what I said to the nurse.

'Well done.'

What was well done? Her timing? Or just the fact that her ability to get pregnant has coincided with her desire to be so?

I thought I'd done *well*: problem solving, quick thinking, acting practically. I've always been the sensible one. Mature. Adult. Though of course I couldn't tell anyone how well I'd done.

What a contrast to how things had been when we were teenagers, when every night out began with a lecture about contraception, and in our twenties, when we gained respect for our having things to do other than procreate, for our self-control (self-preservation).

'Look at this great maternity dress I got the other day,' she says, flicking through pictures on her phone. 'And I've bought some toys already. This baby is going to feel so loved, so *wanted*.'

Wanted. I thought I knew what everyone wanted. I thought my parents would be disappointed in me. I thought friends would think badly of me for not being married first and planning things together properly. Some women have babies to please someone else. I got rid of mine for the same reason.

Even the nurse hadn't understood. Once I'd told him my age, he literally said, *What's the problem?* As if being 29 was enough.

It's not ideal, I said. I meant it at the time.

'When are you going to start telling people?'

'I want to put it on Facebook,' (of course she did) 'but Joe wants me to wait until we've told everyone face to face. I think he wants to see their reactions.' (To be told *congratulations* again and again, as if it's the greatest achievement in the world.)

A little thought sneaks into my head: what would she say if I said, right now, *I'm pregnant too?* Would she wonder whether my baby was *wanted?* Or would it be *congratulations* too, rather than the doubt and questions I assumed would follow? Maybe she would be happy for me regardless? Maybe I needn't have worried. Maybe I needn't have…

'Why does Joe want to see their reactions? Is there anyone who won't be simply delighted at the news? It's not like it's unexpected, is it?'

She pauses. Have I said something wrong?

'I mean, since you got married last year. That's what most people do, isn't it? Get married and start trying?'

The cloud passes from her face and she moves on. 'I've gone a bit mad buying new clothes, but I figure I deserve it.'

'Yeah.' I smile quickly, I don't want her to see my cynicism.

(Deserve it? What for? Seems the wrong way round: the hard work comes later. But by then no one will be saying *congratulations* – it'll all be about the baby. Let her enjoy it while she can.)

A thought occurs to me, and the conversation pauses while I form my next question. 'Forgive me for asking this,' I begin tentatively, 'I only ask because we're sisters… It *was* planned, wasn't it?'

She blushes.

Three months she'd said they'd been trying. Had that been an outright lie, to make me think that she'd gone about things the 'right' way?

'Well, it wasn't *ideal* timing,' she said. 'But we're happy about it. I... we...'

Another thought, another pause. 'Did you... want it more than him? Were you...'

She screws up her face, then meets my eye and whispers, 'I came off the pill at Christmas. I didn't tell Joe.'

So *she* had been trying for three months.

'And he thinks it was a happy accident?'

'Mmm.' She nods.

Talk about not ideal.

'But I didn't feel we could hang about,' she says by way of excuse, 'I'm 29, after all.' She widens her eyes, realising what she's said – I am three years older. 'But you don't want a baby yet,' she waves the thought away with her hand. 'You've got your job, and your house. You're the serious one.'

As if having a baby isn't serious.

'Yeah,' I reply. 'But I want children someday. When the time is right.'

Janikowksi's Solution

Jim Bell

We all agreed. We needed a big idea. We needed to expand our business. Our company, Stellar Information Systems, served the IT needs of a small client roster. We needed a radical idea to sell to new clients. I felt confident I had the solution. I just had to convince senior management of the marketability of my brainchild. I admit, it represented a revolutionary approach, a big departure from the routine programming Stellar Information performed for existing clients. My idea would enable the company to go after bigger fish.

My heart pounded as if it were about to burst out of my chest as senior members of the IT department filed into the small conference room.

"OK, Janikowski, tell us what you've got," barked Mr. Abernathy, head of IT. Abernathy is a hard man to please. Others in the IT department generally follow his lead.

I swallowed hard, then touched my laptop to begin my pitch.

"Social media is the driving force for communication today. People get their news about politics, the weather, family updates, the daily routines of their friends, primarily through social media channels. One company alone has over 2 billion users worldwide. And it continues to grow every year."

I'm not telling anyone anything new here. Our company devoted much attention to digital space, developing algorithms and writing programs to improve and enhance performance. More clicks, more likes, more shares. Drive numbers higher. It's the goal of our business. It's also the goal of many other companies, making it hard to compete in that space.

I had been looking at a different approach. I had been researching and analyzing patterns of behavior on social media for months. I had found that people share the most intimate information about themselves. But, primarily, they show us the best parts of their lives. They tell us how their lives are superior to ours.

"Get to the point, Janikowski," Abernathy barked.

"Yes, sir." I cleared my throat, then stepped closer to my audience like a lawyer pleading his case to the jury.

"But, what do people *really* share on social networks? They tell you how their children are smarter, more talented, and better-looking than yours. Their achievements are more impressive than yours. It's rare that anyone shares a post about the everyday struggles they face in life."

I could see the curiosity growing on the faces of my audience, bodies shifting in their seats. Social media creates a false reality. It presents an existence where users are overcome with the fear of missing out. It constantly shows us the best of what others have. It generates a perpetual state of envy in its users. People think, *How can he afford that car?* Or, *What's so special about her that she's engaged?* Or, *Why should she be published and not me?* How often do we hear people say, *I thought I knew this person, but I misjudged them,* and then proceed to unfriend or unfollow them. Social media can drive a wedge between friends and bombard us with the haves versus the have-nots. We could use this to our marketing advantage.

"People compete to have the most friends, the most followers, the most likes, the most connections. We compete to have the cutest pictures, the most entertaining videos, the most popular friends. We try to convince others we have better knowledge and insight than they do. We share links and saturate others with information that we think is newsworthy or sensational and in many cases we are unaware of what it actually means. We need to be the first to report the death of a celebrity. Social media can be productive, but it can also have a dark side. We need to alter the constant display of superiority it presents. We need to remind ourselves that the things we envy in others do not lead to happy, fulfilling lives. We need to keep people engaged rather than turn away thinking their lives are a failure."

Yes, now is the time. They are primed and pumped. Their whispers and murmurs are proof of a growing curiosity. They are ready for the big idea.

"And so, I propose that we develop an anti-envy algorithm for use in social media."

Eyebrows shot up stretching to reach hairlines. Heads turned from side to side to gauge reactions on neighbors' faces. They all recognized a revolutionary idea when they heard one.

"The algorithm would monitor the number of posts judged as being *superior* and balance it with posts considered fairly mundane. For example, we might balance a superior post with a post of someone having a quiet evening at home with their cat."

I clearly had them now. Total silence engulfed the room. Dozens of stunned faces stared at me, then turned to Abernathy. He leaned back in his chair, eyes squinting to narrow slits.

*

I'm now sitting across from the head of the IT department at Quantum Digital Solutions. I have so many ideas I want to share with him and his team.

"We'd certainly like to hear some of your thoughts, Mr. Janikowski," he says. "But tell me again, why did Stellar Information Systems terminate your employment?"

The Envious Comic

M Pauseman

Nigel Kores walked onto a badly lit stage. A sole spotlight making a circle no larger than a metre across on the small platform. It could have just been a table lamp cello-taped to the ceiling. As he approached the mic stand, he took in the darkness of the room in front of him. Why was it dark in the room? He was performing an afternoon gig in August. All the windows had thick blackout curtains drawn and the guests were all given tealights on their tables. But not even real tealights. They were battery-powered LED tealights, as there was not a smell, not a flicker of flames and no light smoke wafting in the dark. It was a poor attempt by a poor city centre café to create ambiance.

He cleared his throat. The crowed hushed and stared at him. He could make out the small tables of two or three. There were about fifty people in the room. He began.

Hi, I'm Nigel Kores, and the first thing you should know about me is that I am not funny. So, go ask for your money back now. Hopefully you haven't watched enough of the show for them to complain.

Silence. Nigel shrugged his shoulders and carried on.

It saddens me to look at the world today. Apathy is the drug everyone is hooked on, and while ignorance may be bliss, do you want to ignore the fact that your country is sinking around you?

That got a chuckle.

I ask myself why women can't get home safely. Why must they run in fear and not for fitness? Where is Madam Justice when you need her? She's in Dublin. Anyone in the crowd ever been to Dublin?

More silence.

Well, let me tell you. The castle in Dublin has a representation of Madam Justice who is not blind. Who has her back turned to the people, but faces the power, and her sword is ready to strike anyone whom she sees fit. Because, remember, she is not blindfolded.

A louder chuckle this time. The crowd is warming up.

I can't help but think that no matter what words I use, what I actually say, the thing that will be remembered is the one sentence I use with the intention of satirising the whole situation. Comedy is made to make you laugh, but comedy is deadly serious.

An old hip-hop band, one I hold close to my heart, once said that the revolution will not be televised. And I agree, it won't. Thirty years later, it still won't. The only change I see is that now the revolution has to come with a hashtag in front of it.

Now people are laughing, some even clapping. Finally, a reaction.

I do envy the ignorant. I envy people able to sit back and not give a fuck. I envy those who died fighting for something, in a time where fighting made a difference. I envy people who are capable of laughing at the news instead of getting angry. I envy those who think "The Sun" is news. I envy people who think it is perfectly fine for half-naked women to be on billboards, but want a breastfeeding mother to cover herself. I envy the man who isn't forgotten thanks to the medals on his chest. I envy the writers who came before, the comics of old. I envy the generation who didn't have Facebook. I am an envious man, as you can all see. It isn't bad, I just think being stupid would be easier.

An eruption of laughter.

I want you all to read this in a letter, so my handwriting can show my emotions. So, if the ink was smudged, you would know I had cried. I envy people who have truly loved. I envy people who have truly lived. Nobody will ever answer if there is life after death, but nobody is willing to tell you there is life before death either. So, I ask myself, is this how they keep us under control? Freedom of speech but only if you can pay for it, right? Did you know that there are kids, not much older than 16, locked up in jails in America? Their only crime is being poor. I envy America too. I envy people who can watch someone be executed and think that is justice. That someone else dying is closure. I envy people who find The President funny and not worrying. He would make a great stand-up comedian, don't you think? Because he is a joke. I envy the people who live on memories of the past, thinking that one great moment in time can be lived again. I envy you, for being sat down while I am stood up here. So, enjoy that while you can.

The crowd gave Nigel Kores a standing ovation on his first ever gig, in a shitty café in a city centre somewhere in the UK.

Charlie's Girls

Chloe Timms

I spy between the gap in the curtains. Charlie's sat at the front of the stage on one of the round tables, best view in the house, two fingers perched over the rim of his glass. His fingers aren't sat there to say, "You can take the glass when I'm good and ready", it's to make a point: I own the place. He's on his own, sat in a sad crumpled suit that's been hung against the frosted-up window of his car, pine-scented. If you listen to the girls in the dressing room, the wife burnt all his other suits. That's only half of it. She got his credit cards too, and that gotta hurt. One of the girls, Miss DeeDee, says she feels sorry for him, but she's young, still new. Still buys tatty wigs from grubby corners of the internet and can't get her contouring straight. Shame. The other girls say she don't know what Charlie's about yet. Don't know he likes to come into the dressing room after the show with a bottle of fizzy wine and call it champagne.

Showtime in ten. Clarissa Tease parks up next to me to steal the light from my mirror. She puckers, pouts. She's been at it longer than I have, thirty years in June, so she keeps saying. She thinks that makes her our mama, bossing us and telling us who can sit in what chair, who can wear red tonight. Only one girl gets to wear red.

'I was doing drag while you girls were still crying for your mamas,' she says.

'And it shows,' says Viva, of the other girls. She mouths 'saggy' but doesn't keep it quiet. She's asking for a smack.

The room hollers, then coos quiet just as quick when Clarissa spins back the chair. She has the dress, the heels and the face full of setting spray, but her aim's good, her fist hurts. She says Charlie found out the hard way once, but it's hard to imagine Charlie trying it on with a big girl like Clarissa.

Viva unfolds her legs unbothered. She still hasn't found her shoes or fitted her wig, her ratty boy hair showing underneath. I wish Charlie stopped by the dressing room before the show started.

Showtime in five. Miss DeeDee's practising her strut: up and down, sway, up and down. Some of us watch, clap. We wanted the same treatment ten years ago when we were starting out, ignoring them older girls who'd seen it all before, knew better.

We used to take it in turns to wear red, perform the big number at the end. We'd draw straws if there were any disputes. Headlocks, too heavy to be called catfights. The starring role gets you the biggest bucks at the end of the night, a flutter of notes tossed onto the stage. If you're lucky there's a guy in the crowd with a business card who knows someone that knows someone in the big bars. We don't draw lots no more. Now it's Charlie's pick. His choice of girl. It's been Viva five weeks on the trot.

Me and Charlie were pressed up in his car and I asked about it. His wife didn't know everything then, so he was fielding her calls, half an eye on his phone while his hand crept up my thigh. I wanted to talk first. He didn't much like that part.

'Viva needs the practise,' he said.

I toned down my language in Charlie's car. 'She been practising for weeks now. Customers'll stop coming if it's the same queen performing the same damn song every week.'

'And what do you know about what the customers want?'

I knew it didn't take much to flip him between moods. Guys have buttons too. He forgot I knew that. I put my hand on his chest, new lacquered nails, and apologised, told him what a girl would say. He kissed me on the mouth, told me I could sing next time.

Showtime in two. Viva's found the shoes, accused me of moving them. She won't put them on before the curtain's up. She's superstitious like that. The height of them heels – Clarissa said Viva'd be lucky not to break her neck one of them days. Course, we all have our own rituals before we line up on stage. Hail Marys for one, whisky shots for another. Me? The full lyrics to Madonna's Vogue under my breath without a single mistake, one wrong word and something bad will happen. I know it.

'Boss's in tonight girls,' Clarissa says, telling the room what I already know. She gives Viva a theatrical wink. I powder my face.

'Can't blame a girl, now. He's a free agent.'

Miss DeeDee puts her hands on my shoulders. 'Showtime in one!'

Places girls. Viva wedges into them heels, Miss DeeDee makes the sign of the cross and Clarissa sprays her throat. Vogue vogue vogue.

The lights come up and the whoops and whistles carry us to the front of the stage. Charlie slaps his thigh off-time to the music, pretending he don't know all the words and can't sing along like the rest of the audience. He ain't like them, is he? We each take our turns at the front to blow our kisses, to curtsey.

One of the girls throws a boa into the crowd like a snake, hoping she can retrieve it from one of the pretty boys later.

My heart doesn't thunder much when it's my turn, I been at this too long. Doesn't beat when Charlie don't look in my direction neither. It's when Viva rises on her feet, that's when my heart starts thrashing, when she twirls for her big moment. Spotlight beating down, shutting the rest of us in the dark. It's the shoes I look at, still gleaming from their box, not even fakes. Charlie had them wrapped. Type of shoes that'd cost your whole month's rent, without change.

Viva takes a step forward, like she don't know what's coming, like she ain't expecting what I am, that her heel's gonna snap, send her tumbling, smack off the stage. And someone else is gonna take her place, get given the new heels, and step up to sing. And that someone is gonna be me.

Under Her Bed

Pamela Painter

It happens in our dorm room every night. Before my roommate flops into her skinny bed across from mine, she stoops down, kneels, and peers under her bed. The first night she did this—with me clearly noticing—she looked embarrassed, so I gave a little shrug as if to agree that you never know.

A month later my boyfriend stays over and witnesses the ritual I now take for granted. His arm around me grows tense as my roommate kneels to look under her bed. He narrows his eyes, shakes his head. Next day he says, "Whoa. Aren't you tempted to put something under there: a Trump Halloween mask?" He makes more suggestions: a cactus plant, wet noodles. I tell him to leave her be.

Sometimes when she is in class I try on her bunny slippers whose long silky ears dust our floor. Pink rosebuds sprout on baby doll pajamas tucked under her pillow. Her sheets are a pale spring green. From her shelf, I take down the Ouija board and run my fingers over its face that glows white in our nights like the moon.

Her parents call every day. Her mother has a high, Christian voice; her father's voice is low and lawyerly. Being an only child, I envy her twin brother's frequent visits from his college three hours away. They both have blue eyes set rather far apart, wispy blond hair. He brings her rolls of cookie dough, which she eats top to bottom like an ice-cream cone. "The 'rents are jealous, so they separated us," he tells me. "It isn't like we dress alike, or have our own language," my roommate says. They both laugh and in unison they say, "boo."

Two or three times a week she lays out a spread from her Rider-Waite Tarot deck. Her favorite spreads are the Celtic Cross and the Tetraktys Spread. On Sunday mornings she lays out the Star Guide Spread to assess the present situation. I wonder if it includes me.

Near Halloween, I ask to borrow the Ouija board. She peers up at it then laments that it is no longer active, that long ago she got rid of the planchet. When she is nervous she chews on her hair. Now she pulls a strand into her mouth and says, "The planchet stopped telling the truth." I didn't know the planchet had a name. The next evening the Ouija board is missing.

One morning she insists, "Let me do a reading for you." She is sitting cross-legged on her pink puff—a comforter to me—giggling over the cards. I always tell her "another time." I am fearful of her third eye. I wonder if she is equally fearful of my major in neuro-biology, whose textbooks roam around our room. The time I thumbed through her Tarot deck I saw that the Devil card and a few more were missing. There were two "Wheel of Fortune" cards, two of "The Lovers," and "The Star." The cards are soft, pliant, their edges furred from use. I tell my boyfriend about the missing cards. That is probably why, when she pleads for the umpteenth time, my boyfriend finally lets her read his cards. He moves from my bed to hers. They sit cross-legged, opposite each other. He winks at me as she tells him to cut the deck, then lays out the Star Guide Spread. Clearly, he likes what he hears about his intelligent, virile self.

One night before Thanksgiving break, drunk or stoned, mad at my boyfriend, I slide under her bed and pass out. I wake with her hand on my mouth, but it isn't a hand. It is her mouth saying it was in the cards; she knew it was only a matter of time.

That last part isn't true. What happened is that I passed out on my own bed, drunk or stoned, mad at my boyfriend. It was my boyfriend who crawled under my roommate's bed. It was her mouth on his mouth. Had it only been a matter of time?

Venus Envy

Tim Thompson

Dana was a bit drunk.

She and Niles had chatted their way through a bottle of Riesling over dinner... which was pretty standard. Niles had prepared a delicious meal... a Thai chicken salad. *That* wasn't standard – not that he didn't ever make dinner; he just wasn't normally that... exotic. She was suspicious at first, but the meal was just a new recipe "for a change." Well, she'd certainly drunk to that.

As they stumbled to their bedroom, it was obvious Niles was up for sex. Unusually, she wasn't in the mood – it'd been a busy week, and the food and wine... well, Dana just wanted to go to sleep. After nine years of marriage and two children, Niles still turned her on, but not tonight.

"Why don't you take care of yourself while I check on the kids?" she teased. "That should give you *plenty* of time." She snorted as she laughed... Oh god; she *must* be pissed.

"Oh dear, Dana," he replied with mock seriousness, "you're going to have to do something about that penis envy."

"In your dreams, Niles," she said, playfully pushing him into their bedroom.

Dana snuck down the corridor to Clem's bedroom. Opening the door, the light from the corridor streaked across their five-year-old son's peaceful face. She bent over and kissed him on his forehead. "Sweet dreams, sweet boy."

Lexie sat up as soon as Dana opened the door. Oh no… this was not good, although not entirely unexpected. Their seven-year-old daughter was a firecracker of a child. She had a short fuse that was easy to set off, but she was also dazzling… some of the things she came out with. Lexie was born on July 23, 2011… the day Amy Winehouse died, and Niles and she joked the troubled singer had been reincarnated in their daughter… Dana had even called her Amy on extreme occasions. Weirdly enough, it would sometimes calm her down.

"Mummy!" she whispered urgently.

Oh god, she was wide awake. Niles would definitely have time to look after himself.

"What is it, sweetheart? It's late… you need to be asleep."

"Mummy?" she asked as Dana sat on the edge of the bed.

"Lie down, Lexie," she whispered, gently patting the covers as her daughter snuggled back into her bed.

"Mummy?"

She stroked Lexie's dark (Amy Winehouse) hair, "Yes, sweetheart?"

"What's penis envy?"

The hair stroking stopped. Omg! "Sleep time now, Lexie, you've got show and tell at school tomorrow."

"Is something wrong with Daddy's penis?"

"No! Of course not!" This was not good… her Riesling head wasn't ready for this. Trying to sound reassuring, she added, "Daddy's penis is fine, now close your eyes."

"But I heard Daddy say penis envy, and he sounded sad."

"Lexie," she said more sternly, "there's nothing wrong with Daddy's penis."

"Don't you care about Daddy?"

"What? Of course I do."

"But you told him he had to take care of it himself."

"Daddy's a big boy, sweetheart." Riesling had replaced reasoning.

"But why did he have to take care of it?"

Oh for god's sake, what sort of conversation was *this*? "That's enough, Lexie. Time for sleep." She kissed her daughter's head and tucked in the blankets. "Now, goodnight."

Niles laughed when Dana told him about her conversation with Lexie. "That'll teach you to ignore my penis."

She'd thrown the last makeup-stained cotton ball in the bin and was just about to collapse into bed when their bedroom door opened and in walked Lexie. Niles was already under the covers, checking emails on his phone. "What's the matter, Lexie?" he asked, scrolling down the screen; she was always getting out of bed and coming into their room. What she hardly ever did was burst into tears. "I'm worried about your penis, Daddy!" she cried.

"Oh god," Dana said under her breath.

Niles' answer to Lexie's outburst was to sit her on the bed between them and explain to her what she'd *actually* heard. "Firstly, there's nothing wrong with my penis, okay?" Lexie nodded, chewing her lip. "What I said to Mummy was that *she* had *Venus* envy."

(Omg, what was Niles playing at?)

Lexie quickly turned to face her. "Do you, Mummy? *Do* you have Venus envy?"

How the hell was she supposed to answer that? "I doubt it, sweetheart."

Lexie looked confused and turned back to Niles. "What's Venus envy, Daddy?"

(Yes, Niles, what *is* Venus envy?)

"Well, Venus is a planet like the Earth."

"I know that," Lexie snapped, "what's envy?"

"It's wishing you had something that someone else has."

"Why do you wish you had Venus, Mummy? And who has it?"

Dana raised an eyebrow at her husband. "Good questions, Lexie."

Niles had to think for moment, "Weellll… Venus is a beautiful planet," he began; "not as beautiful as Earth, but much more beautiful than Mars. And it's the people from Mars who have Venus envy."

(*Really*, Niles?)

"But Mummy doesn't live on Mars."

(No, that's *men*.)

"Not now, but she used to."

(What?)

"*Did* you, Mummy? Did you live on Mars?"

"Niles, this is ridic–"

"Mummy can't remember, sweetheart; she was only a baby when she came to Earth."

"That's enough, Niles." This could go on forever, and, judging by her sly grin, Lexie wasn't buying it anyway; she just wanted to stay in their bed.

But Niles carried on. "And do you know that people who come from Mars are green?"

Lexie shook her head.

Dana rolled her eyes.

Niles nodded. "Mummy was a green baby."

Lexie began laughing. "That's not true, Daddy."

"Of course it is!" Niles teased, "If someone really wants what someone else has, they are considered *green* with envy."

Dana had had enough, "Okay you two, do you *really* want to know what makes me green with envy."

"Earth!" shouted Lexie. Oh god; she was wired now.

"No, Lexie," she said seriously; "Mums who have daughters who go-to-sleep-and-stay-in-their-beds, and husbands who know what's good for their penises."

The Key

Michael Webb

Alice tries to remember who had given her the key, or what the key is doing there, loose among the pens and tissues and lipstick at the bottom of her purse. Alice is sitting by the window, staring out at the reflection her salmon pink shoe makes in the glass. She looked at mirror Alice, sipping at her unsweetened iced tea, the lines her thighs made under her calf length dress, the way her new haircut made her face too angular, too bony and old and maternal. Alice wondered if mirror Alice compared her fading looks to the other women in the locker room after spin class, still measuring, still ranking, still an insecure youth. It wasn't a lie, looking maternal. She was a mom, on her way to pick up her Jacob at hockey practice, but she was still vain enough, at age 49, to still want to not look the part.

Alice travels quite a bit, to seminars, or to meetings, or to visit her sister in Eugene, or to deliver her son to his father once a year, but she had quickly learned to dispose of those plastic hotel keys, after one too many nights when white wine fogged her brain to the point where she couldn't recall which pizza place advertisement was from this week's hotel. She made it a rule at that point – after getting home, you pitch the key. Now here's a rogue, a white plastic card with a Domino's Pizza ad on the back with an area code she couldn't place. Where had this one come from?

The store had the usual collection of students, moms with strollers, and a businessman in a nicely cut suit, having a break, she assumed, between sales calls. The employees were young, moving back and forth briskly, stocking, reshelving, making drinks for the drivethru. Alice watched a blonde short-haired girl reach high to get something off a shelf, and her shirt gapped, showing a sliver of tan skin above her hips. Alice wondered what she was studying in college, what her major was, whether it was a boyfriend or a girlfriend who held her tiny perfect heart.

She was digging for her phone when she found the card, needing to check the time. She had spent her morning on the phone and the laptop, checking on leads, leaving messages, returning emails, until finally deciding to get out of the office and give herself 20 minutes of solitude before the hurricane of the afternoon of child care and dinner and homework and more phone calls. She knew that by the time the Catholic school across the street let out, and a troop or two of uniformed and unformed girls come through, laughing and talking and ordering their low fat drinks, it was time for her to pack up and leave. But since she didn't know when the school was in session and when it wasn't, she needed to check her mental clock, which told her they should be here by now.

The Heedless Ones, she called them, tiny skirts and polo shirts, with a kaleidoscopic variance in body shapes and sizes that somehow still made them look the same. Their thighs were too big, and too visible, their skirts hiked or pinned to the very edge of decency. Alice remembered being horrified at possible exposure of her upper thighs when she was in high school, a fear obviously not shared by today's young people. Their bodies were almost comically perfect – women, but without any scars, without any evidence of achievement, of battles won and lost. She knew they cared about overexposure, to some degree–

female psychology hadn't altered that much – but they threw off the aura of not doing so as readily as the perfume they wore too much of.

She liked to watch them laugh, watch the attention they attract and reject simultaneously. She categorized them, the alpha, the quiet one, the tall one, the big girl, the skinny one. Alice wasn't so old that she didn't remember the tension of those groups – the layers of mistrust and envy and slights that a gaze and a facial expression and a sharp cutting remark would punctuate. The bitterness, the drama, the raw power politics of who liked who that got more rhetorically violent when slow, witless boys entered the calculus. She loved their life, the way they were passionate and full of themselves and sparkling with potential, their thrilling adventures right in front of them, but she didn't envy the new minefields her girlhood never required she cross.

Alice fingered the card, watching the water condense on her iced tea. Was it Houston? Kansas City? Omaha? She watched the Heedless Ones walking across the parking lot, right on time, a tight little group of five, with a boy in a similar polo shirt and slacks trailing a little bit behind. She watched him look at them, the expressions of fear and joy and lust chasing each other around his little peach fuzzed face. They approached the door, the pretty one, who Alice assumed was the alpha female, yanking it open with too much force, allowing the whole crew to crowd into the small space. Their voices were loud and tinny, suddenly bottled by the walls and ceiling.

Alice stood, arranging her dress around herself, still eyeing the teenagers as they diffused towards the counter. Alice wondered who decided that a short skirt was a scholastic outfit, and decided it was probably a man. Alice let them drift away from the door, and then gathered her bag and her iced tea and walked through it herself, on the way to her car and her son and her life. Alice wondered about the mysterious key that she had found, and for a moment, sinking into the seat of her BMW, she wished she had a passionate, heedless story that went with it.

Window

Dan Spencer

Reuben Paris waves in my direction. Reuben Paris drinks zesty little coffees on the pavement after drop-off, sunlight streaming down Argyle St., east to west. Reuben Paris wears wide-legged, cropped trousers and a Patagonia® cap this season: it's summer. Reuben Paris sells photographs and Reuben Paris networks. Reuben Paris is a regular at a Sauchiehall St. bar. If you've been there, he'll have struck up conversation with you.

Reuben Paris has a five year old at my five year old's school. Reuben Paris buys prosecco for our children's teachers: the last day of term. "Hooray for the Paris father!" they sing. I don't disapprove. Reuben Paris' child and my child are becoming friends. Reuben Paris' child and my child are two of the only white girls in the class. Reuben Paris greets me in the playground. Reuben Paris has "the chat". I can't keep up with Reuben Paris.

Reuben Paris has a coffee guy, a hair guy, a fish guy, etc. "What's fresh?" says Reuben Paris. "What do you recommend?" Reuben Paris and his fishmonger are on first-name terms. When Reuben Paris stops by the shop: "Oh, it's Reuben!" When Reuben Paris' fishmonger needs photographs, it's Reuben Paris he thinks of. But did he really need the photographs? Did he think first of the photographs and then of Reuben Paris? Or was Reuben Paris on his mind already? Was he always thinking, "Reuben Paris, Reuben Paris, Reuben, Reuben…" then:

"Why don't we have some photos taken?"

Reuben Paris is a name in the neighbourhood. Reuben Paris is a name at the school. Reuben Paris is an unbelievable name. Reuben Paris is a name I can't really believe in and can't imagine myself having.

I can't keep up with Reuben Paris. But I like the idea of Reuben Paris.

Reuben Paris' fishmonger's is in the bottom of a warehouse on the same road as Reuben Paris' daughter's school (but isn't it also my fishmonger's? Isn't it also my daughter's school?). Reuben Paris schedules the shoot after pick-up. He has my wife go along, too. My wife takes our daughter and Reuben Paris takes his daughter.

Reuben Paris speaks to me in statements. Reuben Paris speaks to me in semaphore. Reuben Paris lifts a placard saying, "!!!" Reuben Paris speaks to me, as I go by, his back against the golden plate glass window of Reuben Paris' coffee shop, a coffee in his hand, a cigarette in his hand. I should say something, but he's lost interest.

Honestly, I like him.

He has my wife enter some of his photos. He has her as a woman buying the evening meal with her daughter in tow. He throws in his own kid for good measure. Reuben Paris' daughter and my daughter are of different heights but have the same haircut, so it's believable they could be sisters. The five year olds flit about, inspecting the beds of ice, the crates, the shelves, the tanks… I think my baby's in the frame, as well.

One day, somebody will find these photographs and assume they're real or assume they're not real. They'll imagine it's their life, it's their wife, looking at my wife. They'll imagine it's their daughters, looking at my daughter and at Reuben

Paris' daughter. They'll find it desirable, and they'll go on looking at it through Reuben Paris' lens.

Out of the blue, Reuben Paris decides to stand a floor lamp by the back wall of the shop. It's so the scene will seem lit by a window, when the truth is there isn't a single window anywhere to be found. But Reuben Paris understands light. Now everything, look, everything – the young mother, the amiable fishmonger, the bright heads of the children and the shiny, wet bodies of the fish – everything seems suddenly awash, suddenly utterly overcome with gorgeous, liquid light.

Months afterwards, however much I rake across the internet, the pictures don't surface.

Prose | Non-Fiction

235	Ivy League Envy	*Dorin Schumacher*
238	Cecilia's Visit	*Melissa Auburn*
242	The inVisible Me & Envy	*Lloyd Simon*
246	A Watch	*Allan J. Wills*
248	Sarah the Stately	*Michael Robinson Morris*
252	Urology	*Jason Arment*
255	All that glitters …	*Jeffrey Weisman*
257	Paris Envy	*Christie Munson Muller*
260	Calvin Klein Thong – 2004	*Stephanie Reents*

Ivy League Envy

Dorin Schumacher

Bobby Gallaway was the sexiest boy in the group I hung out with during the hot, humid summers at our swim club on the north shore of Long Island. He was a tall, full-lipped, blond, blue-eyed guy the other boys submitted to without complaint.

I would have called his intense energy *charisma*, if I'd known the word. Maybe he had nuclear fission inside his body. He was *alive*.

Bobby's father was a heavyset man with a small head who managed the Westchester County airport. His mother looked and talked like the movie star Joan Crawford, with a deep, cigarette smoker's voice. Grace Gallaway mocked herself when she found out she was pregnant with an unexpected third child at the age of forty, but I didn't understand the joke.

Bobby's parents decided to send him to Hotchkiss, a prep school established to help boys get into Yale. He was on the path to success.

I was a junior in public high school, class of 1953. My mother liked the bottle. My father did something in New York City that kept him asleep mornings when I left for school and absent when I came home.

One evening, my girlfriends and the boys sat cross-legged on my living room floor to play Spin-the-Bottle. Bobby sat next to me. The bottle's open mouth pointed right at me. I felt scared when he kissed me the first time. He kissed long and deep and he sweated.

When I was a senior, Bobby unexpectedly invited me to a weekend at Hotchkiss. The school was located in the northwest corner of Connecticut, an area of low mountains and small lakes. The boys' dates were told to bring a dress for the dance and church plus white gloves and a hat. I didn't own the clothes, but I knew the attitude. Act like a snob.

My mother, who always failed me, fell down the stairs and hurt her back so she couldn't take me shopping. She enlisted a frumpy friend who hated lipstick to take me to the dress shop. I didn't know what to pick and she didn't care. She eyed her watch and I wanted to leave. In despair, I grabbed a grey silk dress with big ugly yellow flowers. None of the hats fit and I could hear the frumpy friend's foot tapping across the store. I grabbed a yellow straw hat with a medium brim and black flowers.

All the buildings on the flat plain overlooking the lake were blocky red-brick and conservative. My car pulled up to the large doors of the main campus building where Bobby met me.

He escorted me to my guest room.

"We have a dance tonight. I'll pick you up at 6:00," he said.

I changed. Couldn't look at myself in the mirror.

At the dance, the other girls wore prep uniforms: solid-pastel sheath dresses and pantyhose, which I didn't bring. When I saw their ballet shoes, I wanted to cut off my feet. I envied the girls and their mothers who knew the social codes.

"Here's your dance card," Bobby said. A different name was on every line and his was last. How hard did he have to twist his friends' arms?

The first guy on the card came over, Bobby introduced us and we foxtrotted on the dance floor. My face burned above the dress everyone was too fake polite to mention. The second boy on the list came and we danced.

After church the next day, Bobby took me for a walk by a small ski jump. As we started down the hill holding hands, Bobby started to run. I fell and he dragged me on the ground as he ran. I was sure he was punishing me for the ugly dress.

After I got home, Bobby started dating my best friend. I was overcome with envy. My friend wasn't even pretty, but she was well balanced from the ballet lessons she took.

I didn't blame Bobby. I was a total embarrassment.

As I searched for a way to end the story of humiliation, I googled Robert D. Gallaway and learned that he was an "All-Time Letter Winner" for Yale football in 1952, 1953, 1954, and graduated in 1955. He entered the Marine Corps as a helicopter pilot and came out a captain. He earned a Harvard MBA and had a long series of top executive positions for various commercial airlines.

The 1986 obituary said that Bobby, at fifty-two, died at his home in Manhattan of lung cancer. He was survived by a wife, daughter, his cigarette-smoking Joan Crawford-mother Grace, and two brothers, including the one she gave birth to at the age of forty.

When he died, I was fifty-one, with no Ivy League connections. After early marriage and two babies, it took thirteen years to earn a bachelor's degree. As a "non-traditional" student, I added more years of graduate study at a non-Ivy university. I struggled to find dead-end jobs in university administrations.

Cecilia's Visit

Melissa Auburn

With Dad at the wheel, Mom sat coldly in the passenger side of our maroon four-door sedan. It would be a long ride from Duluth to Minneapolis. If my parents had an argument about the new arrangement, it most likely happened the night before while Clara and I slept. It was June, and my ten-year-old half-sister Cecilia was flying all the way from California to live with us. Dad's ex-wife, Jackie, was going through a rough patch of sorts. I tried to remember Ceci. Pictures had been exchanged in the mail and in them I saw a small-framed girl with long golden curls. She reminded me of what Goldilocks might look like in real life.

Three years had passed since Dad, Mom and I drove cross-country from Gainesville to Santa Cruz to spend time with Ceci. Back then I was three years old and Ceci seven. With Jackie's permission, Ceci joined us camping in the mountains that summer. The enchantment of the Redwood Forest returned to my mind like blurred colors in a dream. Ceci and I spent our days climbing enormous rust-colored tree trunks, shucking cornhusks for dinner, and sleeping in a misshapen tent under the stars. Mom cast our roles – Dad as Captain Hook, Ceci as Peter Pan, and I was Tiger Lily.

In the fall we said our goodbyes. We'd stay in touch. We'd see each other again soon. Ceci returned to her mother in Santa Cruz and we moved to Minnesota. Two years later,

Clara was born. I had a new baby sister. I helped change Clara's diapers, feed her, and wash her in the bathtub. Another year passed and I turned six. I was the big sister. I wondered how things would change with Ceci's visit. Curiosity took over my tongue. I leaned forward in the car.

"Dad, how long will Ceci live with us?" Dad stared straight ahead, blinking a couple of times before replying. "A while."

My year-old sister, Clara, slept beside me as patterns of farm silos and forests moved swiftly before my eyes. Cecilia was coming to live with us. She would get to spend time with her father – with my father. The scenery changed as we drove closer to the airport. Lanes of traffic became crowded. Cars and trucks zigzagged around us. It was busy. I liked things quiet. I wondered if Ceci liked it quiet too. My thoughts were interrupted by a spurt from my mother. The spectacular array of metal skyscrapers boosted her mood. "Look girls. It's the Minneapolis skyline!"

At the airport arrival gate, I stood at Dad's side while Mom held Clara in her arms. Dad stroked my long brown hair and smiled at me then gazed at a slow stream of passengers emerging from a gray porthole. I joined Dad's search scanning faces as they materialized. Would I recognize her? I thought about the photographs again. Abruptly, Dad stood straight up, grinning. "There she is." My eyes locked on a blue-eyed girl wearing a white top and indigo skirt. The girl ran towards my father and squealed.

"Daddy!"

Soon she was right next to me, her small arms encircling Dad. I watched as he lifted her up, squeezed her tight like California citrus and set her down again. Ceci then turned to my mother, Clara, and me – giving each of us an embrace. Her smile glowed sunlight.

On the way to baggage claim Ceci spoke about the flight.

"There was this nice stewardess... and she brought me all kinds of snacks and juice. I drew pictures for you, Dad. I drew some for the stewardess too."

As Ceci handed Dad a few scrolled pieces of paper, I observed the two of them. I noticed how they shared the same eyes and petite sculpted noses. They had the same curly hair though Dad's was black as obsidian and Ceci's blonde. They were both outgoing and quick-witted. I was shy and demure. Dad adored Ceci. A pea-sized pit cut into my stomach.

In the car again, Ceci sat between Clara and me in the back seat. She taught me a game called "slug bug." Ceci pointed at a green car passing in the opposite lane.

"See those cars that are rounded? Those are Volkswagen Beetles... like a bug. If you see a bug first, you turn to the other person and say, *slug bug* and punch them in the arm." Ceci demonstrated by punching my arm hard. I winced with the sting.

It was apparent that Ceci had played this game before and didn't consider that I was younger and weaker. Mom and Dad paid no attention, having their own conversation in the front seat – livelier than their rapport on the way down. In between slug bug games, Ceci talked incessantly.

"I collect koala bears. Do you know what a koala bear is? I have one here. This is Kimberly. She's from my collection. My mom's going to be sending the rest of my koalas in a big brown box. They should be here soon. I can show you all of them. Each of their names start with a 'K'."

I learned a lot about Ceci on the ride home. Aside from collecting stuffed koalas, she loved *Star Wars* and wanted to make light sabers and role play. She'd let me be Princess Leia since I had brown eyes and brown hair. She would teach me to play card games and chess. She would read me stories and help me pick out my clothes.

By the time we returned to Duluth, my head was spinning, and my arm was sore. At home, that evening, everyone gathered in the living room – Ceci still talking, still the center of attention. I meandered to my bedroom to play with my dollhouse. For a few moments, it was silent. I could think my own thoughts again. I wondered how long Ceci would be staying with us.

I didn't know it would be two years.

The inVisible Me & Envy

Lloyd Simon

Envy. Envy! What does the word evoke in you?

For me, Envy = ☹.

It is the feeling I have that I missed out on much of the potential of my life.

And society has missed out on my full potential.

You see, I'm an inVisible Me. One of the inVisible Generation. Those of us who grew up without knowing who we were. We struggled through life, school, work (for those lucky enough!). Envious of everyone else who seemed to find doing and experiencing these things with so much ease, and yet for us are such struggles.

We're smart.

Often very very smart, but we struggle doing normal things. Society things. Sports. Dating. Socialising. All are foreign to us. And yet we're expected to fit in to society. Our envy leads us to mimic. And so we wear a mask, pretend to be someone we're not, pretend to be "normal". Pretend that everything is okay, when it's not. We learnt through painful incidents that people don't want to really know how you feel, what you think, your ideas. You're labelled 'crazy', a misfit who is weird, quirky, and just doesn't get 'it'.

Nowadays there are more and more of us becoming aware of who we really are, usually as a result of a breakdown, severe depression, or more commonly, suicide attempts. You see, the inVisible Me is 9 times more likely to die from suicide than a neurotypical person. And we're 28 times more likely to exhibit suicidal thoughts. Oh, and one more: suicide is the leading cause of premature death for us … and yet, this is not widely known, and even less is done to help us. Well, nothing is done to help us. We're a hindrance on society.

So who am I?

Have a guess: a generation of people (male and female) in all walks of life, society, countries, and regions, who are all struggling with their identity, have previously been locked up in mental institutions, and subjected to horrific "conversion" therapies.

Many organisations that proclaim to advocate on our behalf and receive many millions and billions in funding in actuality provide no assistance for us, and our voices are not heard or listened to. We are advocated to, rather than being advocates with some say in the way we are treated.

So who am I?

Autistic.

I'm autistic.

But I'm not a child you say. And only children "have autism" … yeah, as soon as you turn 18 it disappears!

To clarify: I'm over 45 years old, I grew up in the 'Rain Man' generation of autism. The generation where we just had to get by and fit in to society. Those of us who were bullied at school and at work, if we were lucky enough to mask enough to get a job. We grew up feeling lost and alone, misfits. We struggled through school, many of us didn't make it. Most of us tuned out and did just enough to get by… but if our potential had been recognised and tapped. OMG! How we could contribute to society if our needs had been understood! Those of us who forged our own way, were allowed to run with our 'weird' behaviours, succeeded in ways that people would not have imagined, and have shaped our society in so many ways. But there are many, many more of us who are hidden away. Hidden behind masks.

The new generation of Spectrumites (uSpectrumites) are now being recognised early enough to get assistance, which is great. But what about the inVisible Generation? Those of us who grew up not knowing who we were, those of us who did things differently, and were so misunderstood. We didn't "grow out of the autism," we just learned to mask ourselves. Pretend to be people we weren't. Some of us are really good at this, and are such good actors that we can still get by. Still wear the mask, pretending that everything is okay. But envious of the New Generation of Spectrumites and the assistance they get.

Deep down, we're struggling, and killing ourselves when it all becomes too much.

We present ourselves to the medical experts, begging and pleading for help, but the traditional methods of addressing severe depression and suicidal tendencies for neurotypical people don't work for us. Anti-depressants? ... don't work for someone suffering from autistic burnout. CBT? ... research has shown that this does not work for those on the Spectrum. And please don't talk about ABA, or bleach enemas! OMG! There is nothing.

Understanding.

Respect.

Simple things, which would make our lives so much more tolerable. Not having to pretend. Not having to wear that damn mask anymore. To be who we are. To do things the way that works for us, and allow us to achieve fantastic things. To be understood. To be listened to. We don't want a 'cure'. We're not puzzle pieces, people who "aren't complete" until someone finds "the missing piece" and makes us "all better".

Let us do things the way that works for us, get out of our way and let us take great strides.

Then the Envy is turned around. All of a sudden, society is envious of us! Of our achievements. Of our way of thinking.

So, that is Envy. The lost life, lost potential. The sadness that I'm not like the 99%, and never will be. After 50+ years I don't think I'm going to change the way I think or experience things, so rather than trying to change me, perhaps now I have permission to be myself, put down the mask, and have a go at some of my crazy ideas for how to change the world. Let me do it my way, and society as a whole will benefit. Society as a whole will become the envious ones ☺.

We are not burdens. With some minor accommodations, we can flourish, and change the world for the better.

We can harness 'Envy' and sadness, and focus on improving things for all Spectrumites.

A Watch

Allan J. Wills

Death sits on the end of my father's bed and sometimes in the night he sees him there. At 91 he might envy Death, that paragon of certainty, as an alternative to the confusion and doubts about where and what year the morning represents, the immobilising pain of ruined knees and the tedious pain of cantankerous bowels. But I don't think there is envy, as occasional ripples of buoyant humour punctuate his general lassitude.

He has a watch in his wardrobe at home. A gold dress watch, as distinct from the battered but practical Olma bimatic shockproof, dustproof, and water-resistant watch he wore to work as a sheet metal fabricator. The Olma is still functioning and responds to a couple of winds, though its plating is corroded in patches from the fumes of hydrochloric acid he used to prepare metals for soldering. By contrast, the gold watch was rarely worn and is bright like new, though overwound and not functioning. His parents presented the gold watch to him in appreciation of his funding a trip for them to his elder brother's wedding. Substantial gifts, in the context of their austere life in retirement in a four-room corrugated iron shack.

I used to sneak into his bedroom and take the gold watch out and look at it when I was a little boy. It is a small watch, more suitable for a teenage boy or girl. You would recognise the case as rose gold, an alloy of copper and gold, fashionable to some these days. The watch was made in the 1950s by Rega, an Israeli company whose specialty in more affluent times became Mickey Mouse and novelty watches with oscillating googly eyes.

As I am his eldest son, my father will bequeath me a secret treasure, a broken gold watch that, had it been assembled with different hands and a different face, would be a wildly gesticulating cartoon mouse, a surprise and delight to any child. But I do not dream of what might have been. In the world of that simple watch, love and best wishes are real.

I know this of my father: He loved me and wished for me opportunities not available to himself. He gave me my first employment in his workshop as an assistant. The wages I earned funded my accommodation while attending university. A pathway to a life he could not imagine.

For this month of summer holidays, I shower and shave him in the mornings when the nurses are busy and visit him in the evenings before bedtime. He recognises me and assures me I am a good son. I could not have wished for a better father and I say so to him. When the holidays end, I will return to work in a distant city and he will be left in the care of others. The nurses urge me to come again sooner rather than later. They know his past memory is sound for now but they will be strangers anew every morning.

Sarah the Stately

Michael Robinson Morris

As far as I knew, our childhood had been carrying on as normal until Grampy died back east. The whole family piled into a car, into an airplane, then into another car or two to get to the Rhode Island funeral. Amidst the gathering of strange relatives around the pastoral grounds of a cemetery dotted with ancient headstones, my cousins Richie and Robbie both wore gray suits and ties that fit their 11- and 13-year-old frames perfectly. My brother David wore the shabby semblance of a suit too—rumpled khakis and an oversized brown jacket. All I had was a pair of green corduroy pants and a yellow patterned short-sleeve shirt. I felt stupid. My dad said not to worry about it.

He chose not to worry about it so expertly that he left us five weeks later. Our family had returned back home to California in time for the fall school year when my Uncle Dick, Richie and Robbie's dad, caught me answering the phone.

"Mike? Can you tell your mother that Grammy passed away last night?"

I didn't know where my mother was to tell her that her mom just died right on the heels of her father. Dad arrived home from work to take me to a Toshiro Mifune movie. We were running late. He told me to just write down Uncle Dick's message on a scrap of paper. I left her a note on the counter that simply read:

"Grammy died."

By the time we got back from the movie, our family was pretty much over. Sobbing and shaken to her foundation after having just lost both her parents in a span of 45 days, my mother made the flight arrangements to attend her mother's funeral—alone. Who can say what hushed arguments and repressed fights went on behind closed doors. All I know is that it was on this solo trip that my dad called our mother long distance to say he wanted a divorce.

That's when the sobbing really kicked in. That's when my mother's duties as a mother went on pause. That's when my brother's childhood went on pause. Both her parents now gone and her husband divorcing her. In her young whirlwind days she had left a privileged life in Perryville, Rhode Island, and bounded to the west coast to hitch up with a blond boy from Newport Beach, whose father sold real estate to Hollywood movie stars like Humphrey Bogart. Now stranded in California, the land of dreamers and entertainers, she had nothing left but her two boys just preparing to enter adolescence. Our world had fallen apart.

But I had someone to fall back on. Sarah Chase was the love of my life—in fourth grade elementary school. Nothing else could be done for me. Mr. Pfeiffer situated our desks in blocks so that my island faced me away from Sarah. But yet I turned to look over my shoulder at her whenever it wasn't obvious. This time she found a stray hair on her desk. As if she were a great Egyptian pharaoh queen she daintily picked up the stray hair with two pincer fingers and slowly, ceremoniously crane-lifted the tiny strand to remove it from her gracious presence. But I did not see this private act of hers as arrogant, stuffy or showy. It was an act both distinguished and funny. It was devastating. How I envied her stateliness! I dreaded I would be next. That I was an ant on her desk and she would ceremoniously dispose of me with her pincer fingers.

Her teeth were blinding white, an emblem of goodness and purity. My teeth were yellow. During my most formative years, nobody told me to brush my teeth before bed. Dad was gone. Mom was still sobbing into her pillow. My brother would get home from junior high school, prematurely thrust into the parenting role of soothing her grief, stroking her forehead as she muttered things like "I'm so confused" and "I just don't know anything anymore." He soon stopped going to school at all. The kids sensed a wounded animal and sought to remove him from the pack by jeering and hazing him. He stopped attending and nobody noticed. He would ride the school bus but then just disappear around some corner and hang out at an arcade all day. Absence letters piled up at home but there was nobody there to read them. Mom was still crying.

But Sarah with her bobbed caramel brown hair and her perfect white teeth—I had determined that she was going to save me. I didn't care if she had heard how I swung blindly at the laughers who tapped me on the shoulder from behind, who knew I was a ticking time bomb, and wanted to show their friends a little entertainment.

But like in Ray Bradbury's story "All Summer in a Day" where the sun only comes out for one day every seven years, Sarah–out of the blue–lavished me with her attention the one day her parents picked her up late and let us play four-square ball in the upper field. It was the most glorious day ever, like we were alone in the universe together. I thought my life was settled, that our marriage and family plans would all be worked out in advance, that my family life would be perfect this next time. At the end of that day when my sun went down, the sky turned dark and overcast. Sarah continued ignoring me for the rest of our lives together. She must have sensed I was a chaos kid.

I was glad we weren't forced to go to my grandmother's funeral, the final ceremony that cut my mother off from her own childhood. Sometimes it is good and healthy to say goodbye in your own way. But for me–I was just glad I didn't have to stand in that pastoral field dressed in ill-matching colors while I envied Richie and Robbie's perfectly-fitting gray suits.

Urology

Jason Arment

In early June I finally got around to scheduling my vasectomy for late August—ostensibly. The VA hospital was in the middle of moving from their long-held location adjacent Rose Medical Center by City Park, to out by the University Hospital on the east side of town. The appointment wasn't set in stone, as the VA's Urology Department disappeared during the move and the VA Choice Program was supposed to call me. But they didn't, not until early December.

Between June and December I saw my primary care doctor to satisfy the VA's requirement regarding the need to have the idea of permanence explained to me, a former Marine with three fourths of his body covered in tattoos. My primary care doc said he didn't know why they'd told me to schedule with him, asked me how I was, and sent me on my way.

I waited until August to harass the Choice Program, who finally scheduled me with Urology at the University Hospital. A few weeks later, two weeks out from sterilization, I got a call from the University Hospital telling me that the form the VA used was about to expire, and I'd need to reschedule. It took a few weeks for me to straighten it all out, and then I was rescheduled for December.

When I finally arrived at my appointment, seven months after I first embarked on my quest, I was informed it was an intake of sorts. I would again talk to a doctor about permanence, but this time it would be followed by a short film I watched on the doc's laptop. The final appointment was scheduled for January, eight months after I started requesting the operation.

The doc was a good guy—erudite, well-spoken, good-humored—but just a little too prim and proper to mask his religious leanings. He was an hour and a half late for my appointment, but I didn't mind. I'd waited eight months: what was another couple hours?

All my nerves failed me when I was back flat against the operating table. The doc numbed my junk then sliced a little hole in my ballsack. I could feel myself starting to crack and wondered if backing out now was even an option. I had to really do something, so I did what I often do when cornered—confront. As the doc was just slipping his tools in my scrotum, I made my move.

"Doc, what's the worst thing you've ever done," I asked. "As a doc. What's the worst you've ever messed up?"

I sort of wanted to ask if he'd ever killed anyone, but as a urologist the chances seemed slim, and civilians get all weird about killing.

"Well I, uh," doc said. "It's been awhile since I botched a vasectomy."

"No, your whole career," I quickly interjected. "Worst thing ever. You won't say because you're in my ballsack?"

"I can't tell you," he said. "I need to concentrate, and I'm not here to think about how I messed up. I'm here to do this right."

"Good thinking, doc!" I said. "I like it. Positive thinking. That's real good."

And so the operation continued. The nurse and I chatted about Sweeney Todd and other gruesome oddities, the highlight being George Washington pulling out his slaves' teeth and undergoing operations to have them implanted in his gums.

"That sounds, well, like a disturbed man with serious smile envy," the doc said, while he worked on my nuts.

"Were people back then just way crazier than I realized?" I asked.

"I tell you what," the doc said. "People are still like that today."

All that glitters …

Jeffrey Weisman

Feelings of envy occur over time. Some people and events make you envious. Others create no envy at all.

For instance, how can you not envy a doctor friend who lives in a three-story ten-bedroom mansion? He has four attractive accomplished children. He always drives the latest car, whether a Corvette or a Lexus or a Mercedes. He takes regular vacations to exotic places.

And though I succeeded in my career, I could never compare to this doctor. Yet even with my pangs of envy, I always saw my life as more successful.

The doctor's marriage had far more tension than mine. His streak of selfishness contributed to an air of marital apprehension and discord. He always seemed on the verge of yelling at his wife, let alone smacking her.

The doctor's kids, all college educated, seemed to resent him. The oldest, married the first chance she got, moved 500 miles away. Another quickly moved 150 miles away.

The doctor proved a manipulative sort. I remember how he would force an issue. "I know you would not mind doing this or that." How could you say no? Envy and resentment accompanied the request – that he could get away with such brashness.

This doctor always seemed to have a lot of friends. But were they real? He would ingratiate himself with new people, even with my friends. I felt reticent to bring him before my friends, knowing he would overwhelm them.

We had such a long-term friendship so I overlooked his actions. But after time, the sense of envy began to fade. The realization of his true nature exposed itself. I no longer envied him. Rather I saw him for what he was, a selfish pushy arrogant individual.

So what does this story have to do with a treatise about envy? Envy is a form of hostile worship. It can turn admiration into resentment. Our society today has so many "winners" who attract envy. Yet can we truly envy those tech billionaires who lack sensitivity and kindness?

In most cases you will not find the grass greener on the other side. Your envy will not enable you to see the negativity or hardships of the person, certainly not on the surface. The envied doctor above had a tortured marriage. His wife wore dark glasses regularly, suggesting not a fashion statement but having received a slap or two.

Surely I did not envy this part of his life. After a multi-decade friendship, I ended it. The sense of reality made the envy disappear.

So when next you have a sense of envy, look closely at the source. See the person in total, for all their assets and deficiencies. Your sense of envy may just never get started.

Paris Envy

Christie Munson Muller

"We had the best time tonight. I guess our *apéritif* turned into dinner. We laughed a lot and we talked for hours. We have a lot in common," Stéphane gushed.

"Sounds like you two had a good time," I said flatly. "What was she wearing?"

"What? I don't remember. Oh wait, maybe a dress. She was wearing a cute dress, the kind a French woman would wear," he chuckled.

"Well, I'm glad you enjoyed your evening. Are you going to bed now?"

"Oui, I've had too much wine. That woman can drink."

"Okay, glad you made it home safe. I will call you tomorrow night." I hung up the phone and instantly started to stew.

I flashed back to a few months before when Stéphane and I met Brigitte. We stopped for Chinese take-out in Sedona, Arizona. She worked at the busy restaurant. Once we learned she was from France, we struck up a conversation in French and English. At the time, I noticed her natural ability to alternate between the two languages. She seemed intelligent in an unassuming way. We learned Brigitte was French-Vietnamese and co-owned a house with her uncle in a nearby Arizona town. She lived in Paris, but spent time in the U.S. with her uncle. I also remembered she was beautiful.

During one of our almost daily phone calls, Stéphane shared he had connected with Brigitte when she returned from Arizona to Paris. Like a bad dream, his comments about their wonderful dinner haunted me the entire afternoon and into that evening.

Her beauty also haunted me. Brigitte was petite, with exotic dark eyes and beautiful olive skin that seemed to glow. I remembered how her long dark hair was casually tossed to one side, in that perfectly imperfect way French women seem to pull off. She was everything I was not.

At the restaurant she and Stéphane hit it off right away. At the time it didn't bother me. Months later, with Stéphane back in Paris and me in the U.S., I felt a pit in my stomach and couldn't shake the anxious feeling that was taking over.

"Allo?"

"Hi. It's me. I know it's early. I'm glad you're awake," I sniffled.

"Hi. What's happening?" Stéphane said in a sleepy voice. "What time is it there?"

"It's late. I can't sleep. I'm thinking a lot about your dinner with Brigitte and it's bothering me. I know it's nothing but I can't get it out of my mind."

"You know we're just friends. I don't feel that way about her and nothing is going to happen."

"I know but my mind got going and I started to think more about it and now it's taken over," my voice trailed off and I paused. "I feel like you're having a 'female friendship affair'."

"You called me at 6:00am on my day off to tell me that?" He sounded irritated.

"Yes I did. And I was thinking about your friend Nathalie too and now there's another one? And I'm not there. Why do you have so many female friends?"

"Because I enjoy talking to people who are interesting and

positive. I get tired of talking about cars and sex with the guys at work. It's boring," he said.

"It seems you have a special relationship with Brigitte. I want to not like her. I'm either a really understanding girlfriend or I'm fucking stupid! Which is it?"

"You're very understanding," he said laughing under his breath.

"I guess my demon is back," I sighed and loosened the grip on my cell phone.

It's true. I was ruminating and spending time with my demon. That little devil sat comfortably on my shoulder and spoke sweet nothings in my ear, as I sat on the couch in the dark for over an hour before I dialed France.

What if friendship turns into more? This has happened before. I don't have to put up with this from him. These were the thoughts that filled my head while I paced the floor of my quiet and lonely apartment.

"Well, I want to be there next time … when you meet her for dinner, okay?"

"Yes, of course you can meet her. If you were here we would have had dinner together, all three of us. I know you will like her," he said yawning.

"We'll see. Okay, I feel better. You can go back to bed now," I giggled.

"Good night my love." Click. He hung up the phone.

My demon was jealousy who'd brought along her good friend envy. They poisoned my mind and wrenched my gut. Luckily, my demon and her evil friend had left for the night, but I knew they would be back.

Calvin Klein Thong – 2004

Stephanie Reents

When I was young, thongs were rubber flip-flops that we bought at the drug store and wore until our heels scraped the ground. Thongs meant summer: chocolate dip cones from Fanci Freeze, tubing the Boise river, dry heat, nights that stayed light until ten, the smell of charcoal grills, cut grass, rhubarb sauce, and cherry tomatoes warm from the garden, one trip to the waterpark, one trip to the drive-in movie theater, one trip to the Western Idaho State Fair, fireworks. The thong that he – my boyfriend from the ages 33 to 36 – buys me is a small triangle with a strip of fabric no wider than my thumb in the back. *Butt floss.* "What size are you?" he asks, calling me from Macys. "Size eight, or a medium," I say, imagining – hoping for – a sweater or a skirt. Hours later, he thrusts a small plastic bag at me. Inside: three thongs, Calvin Klein, in black, white, and beige stretchy material. No lace. No peekaboo keyhole above the pelvic bone. No bows. A beige thong? "I feel like I've got a wedgie." I look down at the bruised white peaches of my buttocks. "Exactly," my boyfriend says, giving my ass a playful slap. "Your wedgie has given me a woodie."

This is the boyfriend, with red hair, pale skin, and almond-shaped blue eyes that get me every time, who is often mistaken for Conan O'Brian. This is the boyfriend with certain, very specific tastes: tall black leather boots, leather pants, white jeans, thongs. Fetishes? I envy how well he knows what he likes and hate how it makes me feel like a paper doll.

This is the boyfriend who once revived three half-dead, half-drowned chicks by submerging them in hot water. This is the boyfriend who lives with chemistry post-docs in a ramshackle commune complete with goats, chickens, sheep, and a mean-ass goose smack dab in the middle of McMansioned Palo Alto, who makes explosives, limoncello, street drugs (just once), prosciutto-wrapped chicken, vulgar wisecracks, bad music on his electric guitar, patented compounds in a pharmaceutical lab on the Peninsula. He explodes out of bed in the morning. Doesn't drink coffee. Drives like a maniac. He is that kind of man. And in this version of the story, I am the kind of woman who is with that kind of man. Which isn't saying much.

On what occasions do I wear a thong for this boyfriend? For the life of me, I can't remember. I wear the boots, knee-high with silver buckles, nearly every day. I wear the black leather pants to go out dancing at a club in the Mission. I wear the white pants on the vacations we take together (twice to Hawaii, where we nearly kill each other). This is the boyfriend who is practically a wizard, who can look beneath a kitchen or bathroom sink and see endless pyrotechnic possibilities, and yet he can't – for the longest time – propose buying one of the things he likes without referring to the experience of buying it for his last girlfriend, an Italian chemist, and I can't tamp down my response – which isn't jealousy, but rather the feeling that she must be a better version of me, smarter, of course, and with a delicious plump rump never prone to erupting in pimples, a woman capable of making her own spectacular fireworks – not a paper doll like me.

And so my boyfriend lights the fuse, and together, we ignite, and we ignite, and we ignite until there's nothing left to burn.

Also from Pure Slush Books

https://pureslush.com/store/

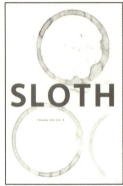

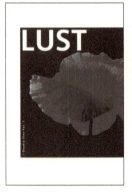
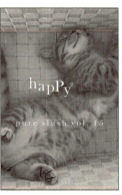

- Wrath 7 Deadly Sins Vol. 5
ISBN: 978-1-925536-68-3 (paperback) / 978-1-925536-69-0 (eBook)
- Sloth 7 Deadly Sins Vol. 4
ISBN: 978-1-925536-66-9 (paperback) / 978-1-925536-67-6 (eBook)
- Greed 7 Deadly Sins Vol. 3
ISBN: 978-1-925536-64-5 (paperback) / 978-1-925536-65-2 (eBook)
- Gluttony 7 Deadly Sins Vol. 2
ISBN: 978-1-925536-54-6 (paperback) / 978-1-925536-55-3 (eBook)
- Lust 7 Deadly Sins Vol. 1
ISBN: 978-1-925536-47-8 (paperback) / 978-1-925536-48-5 (eBook)
- Happy^2 Pure Slush Vol. 15
ISBN: 978-1-925536-39-3 (paperback) / 978-1-925536-40-9 (eBook)